SHADOW FALL: PART ONE

KISSED BY BRIMSTONE BOOK FIVE

LEIGH KELSEY

www.leighkelsey.co.uk

Want an email when new books release - and four freebies?

Join here https://bit.ly/LeighKelseyNL

Or chat with me in my Facebook group: Leigh Kelsey's Paranormal Den

Cover by Carol Marques Cover Design

❀ Created with Vellum

THREE FREEBIES FOR YOU

Fancy some freebies? I'll send you three when you join my newsletter! I promise never to spam you, and I rarely send more frequently than once a fortnight so you won't be overloaded with emails.

Join here: http://bit.ly/LeighKelseyNL

BLURB

I don't want to save the world, I just want my happily ever after.

Gods, mortals, and titans all
  Will bring the end at shadow fall

Those are the words of the prophecy inked on my back, taunting me every time I try to stay away from the world of murder, magic, and misery that Cronus made. We've come too close to death, and I'm ready to throw in the towel, but fate has other ideas. The end is coming no matter what I do, I just don't know whose—Cronus's or mine.

Shadow Fall Part one is the fifth book in the Kissed by Brimstone series, **a spicy paranormal romance for adults** with action, humour, a strong-willed heroine, and psycho archdemon men.

PLAYLIST

GODS by *NewJeans* and *League of Legends*

(On repeat for the entirety of reading the book like I listened to it, on obsessive repeat, for 6 hours every day while writing it. Joking.

(Not joking.))

NOTE

This series contains mentions of past abuse and sexual assault that could be incredibly triggering for some readers, so please proceed with caution. It also contains references to miscarriage. Don't hesitate to skip this book if it's safer for your mental health.

This series also contains some spoilers for the Lili Kazana trilogy, which takes place a year before this series, but only minor spoilers for the events of the story (nothing character-wise is spoiled.)

Leigh x

PART I
PART 1 - VOID

CHAPTER 1

WYNVAIL

*T*hree days ago

As far as final words went, "I'm so obsessed with you," were pretty memorable. I'd given them serious thought, my death creeping up on me slowly, visible and painfully clear. It was far from a sudden death; mine happened slowly and obviously enough to torture me the whole way. I knew I would die, but I was a stupid fool and did it anyway. All because my mate would have been devastated if she lost Wane.

I'd do it all over again because I truly was obsessed with Halwen Vakhara, but it would have been nice to avoid the whole *being unmade and ripped apart until not even dust remained* part. Fuck Cronus. My whole life, I knew I'd only existed because he'd created me, because he was hellbent on freeing himself from his prison, making all his enemies pay, and reinstalling himself as king of fucking everything.

I shouldn't have existed, but he needed a pawn, and I was

given to Cassander Locke in exchange for Wane. Pieces of shit, both of them.[1]

So now I was dead, floating through an endless nothing because apparently made creatures didn't deserve an afterlife. No eternal peace, no realm of pure and ceaseless suffering either. I wasn't sure whether to be relieved or disappointed. Mostly, I was confused that I could still think. I'd been unmade, every atom of my body ripped apart and snuffed out.

So why the fuck was I still *thinking?*

Why did thoughts of Halwen holding me as I died make my chest ache viciously and my hand itch with the need to punch a hole through a wall? Why did I even have a hand? What the fuck?

"Come on," a calm feminine voice murmured. "You're almost there."

Fuck off, I tried to say, the thought of someone other than Halwen speaking to me making me tremble with rage. I might have been dead, but I still belonged entirely to that fearsome, sharp-tongued, violent woman. I was hers. Not whoever the fuck was speaking to me in this black, empty afterlife.

Maybe I'd been dealt eternal suffering after all. Maybe I'd have to endure an endless parade of women who weren't my mate, rubbing salt in the wound of never seeing Halwen again. It sounded like hell.

"He's clinging to death," a deep male voice sighed, and I tried to scowl, tried to grasp my power and split these motherfuckers in two for even daring to come near me.

I didn't want to admit that I was scared. Fuck fear. Just *fuck* fear, and Cronus, and any woman who dared to speak to me who wasn't my beloved.

"What's his name?" the woman asked, her voice subdued and low. There was power in that voice, and it called to me against my will. It pulled me out of the darkness before I could even process it happening. Shit.

"Wynvail," another woman said, equally unfamiliar. Softer, raspier.

"Wynvail," the powerful woman murmured, her voice wrapping around me like a coiled whip, like a net. Trapping me in her grasp. It made no sense. I was dead. Unmade.

"You need to come back. Your soul is struggling; it wants to stay in the darkness. But if *you* want to come out of the dark, all you have to do is follow my voice."

My head spun. I shouldn't have even *had* a head. And I swore the darkness lightened from true void to filmy grey. Fuck, what was she doing? What did these people want with me?

"You're being too vague and poetic, my love," the deep male voice murmured, so much affection in his voice that it made my chest ache fiercer.

I died in Halwen's arms, and as much as that made me feel warm and wanted for once in my miserable existence, I wanted to go back there.

Don't you dare leave. Don't you fucking dare.

Cronus ripped me away from her. Was she okay? Was she heartbroken? The selfish part of me—the majority—wanted her to grieve me. Miss me.

I wanted to matter to the woman who consumed my every waking and dying thought. She was burned into my heart, embedded in every cell of my body, written into the very fabric of my soul. Not that I should have *had* a soul.

"Listen closely," the man said, his voice closer, louder. It echoed in a way that made me tremble inside the dark space my soul cowered within. "You're dead."

No shit.

"Your soul is clinging to death because that's the natural way of things, but you have a choice here. You can stay dead if you choose; just let go and float into the darkness. But if you want another shot, if you want to see your loved ones again, if you want *revenge*, claw your way back to the world of the living. Follow my voice, follow my wife's voice. We'll guide you back."

What. The. Fuck?

My head spun, and as far as I knew I didn't even have a head. Cronus had crushed it into ash and nothingness.

"You have to come back," the second woman said, her raspy voice harder than the other, iron in her words. "Haley needs you. She's falling apart. You have to come back."

The darkness lightened, their voices louder. Those words echoed around my head, making me flinch with every pass.

She's falling apart.

Haley needs you.

How? I tried to ask, and when that didn't work, I tried to scream it. *How do I come back? How do I claw my way out?*

Death was nice and all,[2] but no fucking way was I staying when I had a second chance. I didn't know *how* when I didn't technically exist and I hadn't realised I had a soul to begin with, but I wasn't about to pass up this opportunity.

Unless this was an elaborate scheme by Cronus. It wouldn't surprise me. That bastard was cunning and cruel. It was very on brand for him to give me everything and then rip it away. I'd had a mate who didn't look at me with pure hatred anymore, a mate who held me at my weakest and murmured reassurances, who saw *me* and not the value I had as a tool.

Haley needs you.

She's falling apart.

"That's it," the powerful woman encouraged, her magic rippling through the dark space.[3] "Fight it. You're strong, Wynvail. You have one of the strongest souls I've ever seen."

"Keep talking about his mate," the man murmured.

"I don't want to torture him," the raspy woman sighed. Younger than the powerful woman.

Torture me? Why would she torture me by talking about

my Halwen? Panic and rage fused inside me. What had happened? Was she okay? Had Cronus come for her after he unmade me?

A roar came from deep in the chest I wasn't supposed to have, and I slashed through the darkness, pulling on my magic —*where the fuck was my magic?*

"Almost here," the powerful woman said, coaxing me further out of the dark with her voice. Magic wrapped around me, tingling against my skin, and the emptiness around me filled in with shapes and muted colour. Not shadows but— was that a fucking wardrobe? "That's it, Wynvail."

"Think of your mate," the man said, low and rumbling. "She needs you."

"She—" the younger woman said haltingly. "She broke down in tears earlier. She was a mess—"

I shattered the death clinging to me with a bellowing howl of rage, surging up and grabbing the shoulder of the scarred, brunette woman hovering beside—my bed? It didn't matter where I was or how I was here, or how I had a body when it had been ripped apart to dust.

"What happened to my mate? *Where is she?*"

My yell echoed off the wood-panelled walls of the small room.

"Easy," the man warned, his voice deeper, foreboding. Chills froze my skin, and I snapped my gaze to a tall, black-haired fifty-something man. He hovered at my bedside, and my soul jolted against the unfamiliar confines of my body when his hand came down on my wrist and broke my grip on the brunette young woman. "She's the only reason you're still alive, so I'd treat her better if I were you."

The woman with pure power in her voice turned out to be a graceful redhead in her thirties with a porcelain face, elegant freckled features, and leather armour that criss-crossed over a deep forest green dress. Huh. I was expecting someone bigger, rougher. She might have a soft, careful voice but her aura was *full* of magic.

I shuddered, scrambling up the bed to put my back to the wooden headboard. I scowled, just to preserve some of my dignity, as if I wasn't terrified.

"Wynvail," the brunette said, snagging my attention. She didn't baulk under my glare, but her dark wings ruffled in irritation or concern. I'd never been good at understanding the body language of wings. "Haley's my friend, I'm Lili. She might have spoken about me."

"Liliana, Queen of Hell," the redhead corrected with a gleam in her eyes.

"And the Justice of Hell. The Balance who terrifies even the gods," the man added proudly.

My stomach knotted. "How the fuck am I alive, and what do you want from me?"

I might as well get the bullshit out of the way first. If I was expected to be their pawn or slave, I'd rather know now instead of letting the first taste of freedom give me hope. But fuck, I really felt alive. I was in a homely little bedroom, surrounded by powerful people, and none of it made sense, but I could *breathe,* and my heart thumped my ribs, and I could even wiggle my toes.

"I asked them to save you," the queen and balance and whatever the fuck else said, giving me a tentative smile. "Haley's my friend, and it's not right that you were killed just because you freed her other mate from being tortured for a hundred years. Plus, there's Cronus to consider."

I stiffened, my chest tightening. I locked down my expression, not letting a single emotion show. "What about him?"

Lili sighed, running a hand through her long wavy hair. "He's dangerous, and he's starting a war. We want to stop it before it can begin, and—you know him. You might be able to help us stop him. You were killed unnaturally, and you never should have died—"

"I never should have lived," I drawled, scanning the bedroom and baffled by the normality of it. There were knickknacks on shelves, a chest of drawers that overflowed clothes against the wall, and a worn little rug on the wooden floor. Family photos hung on the walls. I'd been resurrected in a completely normal bedroom. So ordinary it was almost boring. *What the fuck?*

"But you are living," the redhead said, smiling disarmingly. I knew she could blast me into pieces, yet she looked harmless. "And you're strong enough to stay that way."

"It won't be easy," the tall man added, his arms crossed over his dark, elegant clothes—a blend of tailored modern styles in his shirt and classic leather armour in his trousers and boots. "You'll have to regain your strength; your previous body was obliterated, so this one is new."

"What?" I snarled, surging off the bed and stumbling over to the mirror I'd spotted hanging on the wall. I grabbed the dresser when my knees buckled, and scanned my reflection, my shoulders slumping in relief when I saw the same face as always. Same arrogant curve of my mouth, same severe slope of my nose and brutal line of my jaw, even the same narrowed eyes, blazing silver fire. No, that was panic. Because I'd had a scar on my chin, and now the skin was smooth and unblemished.

"Your soul dictates your appearance," he went on, watching me closely, "so you should look exactly the same. You might notice the absence of some scars, tattoos, and other marks. But you're alive."

"This makes no fucking sense," I spat, staring at myself, my mouth opening and closing. "I was *unmade.* How the fuck am I alive?"

I gave the man a wary glance when he came closer, my

soul *quailing* at his nearness. Fucking hell, he was even more powerful than the redhead; he just kept his power buried. When he smiled, I nearly pissed myself.

"I'm Hades, god of the dead and king of the underworld."

My knees buckled. I laughed, a short, staccato burst of sound. He was lying. He had to be. There was no fucking chance this was—

But my eyes drifted to the freckled redhead and my stomach dropped. This was insane. Completely and utterly insane.

The goddess of spring and queen of the fucking underworld waved at me. "I'm Persephone."

"I know exactly what you're feeling," Lili laughed, a smile curving her cheeks.

I was in a tiny bedroom with the god of the dead, the goddess of spring, and the queen of Hell. No, she really didn't know what I was feeling.

"So what do you want?" I breathed. Panic laid its noose lovingly around my throat, tightening in increments until I couldn't breathe.

"Stay here, heal," Persephone replied with a gleam in her eyes. "And when you're well enough, reunite with the mate who's prophesied to kill Cronus once and for all."

I blinked. "And the rest."

"That's all," Hades said, slanting a look at me as I held onto the dresser a little too hard. My knees were weak as shit and I wasn't convinced it was entirely the shock of being in the same room as gods. My body was *new*. "This new war started in Alphaven in *Hell*, the realm ruled by my daughter—" He glanced warmly at Lili. "And home to three of my sons. Whatever plans Cronus has, they involve Hell. And my family."

Hades glanced away, and I frowned. What was he keeping out?

Persephone unfolded from the bed and crossed the small

room to her husband. She took his hand, her eyes only for him. "We'll stop him. I promise, Hades. We'll stop him."

Oh, shit. I'd forgotten my mythology for a moment.[4] Cronus was Hades's father.

"My mate," I said, moving to the small window and gripping the frame so my weak legs didn't drop me on my ass, "is Rhea's descendant." I wouldn't tell him the rest, wouldn't tell him about his mother's suicide. "She's your family."

"Shit," Lili breathed, blinking. "That means she's my family, too."

Sure, whatever. Back to my point.

"She's your family," I said to Hades, my voice cold, "so I'm hoping that makes you inclined to protect her. Keep her safe from whatever Cronus is planning, and I'll do what you want. Ask anything; I don't give a shit. But Cronus doesn't touch a single fucking hair on her head. And I need something else. I'm willing to bargain for it."

Hades glanced at me, weighing me in a way that made my stomach knot. "The only thing I expect of you is to ally against Cronus. Fight with us. I'd protect her anyway because she's my daughter's friend, and she has the power to kill Cronus."

"And it's the right thing to do," Persephone pointed out wryly.

"So you brought me back," I said slowly, "because I might come in handy fighting Cronus."

"We brought you back," Hades said, arms crossing over his chest, "because Cronus is free and has the entirety of Olympus imprisoned under the mountain. He's devoured fifty god descendants and amassed untold power, and he'll only grow more dangerous in the days to come.

All the blood drained from my face, and it was a miracle to even have blood, to have a face but—

"Great," I drawled. "You brought me back to die."

CHAPTER 2

*N*ow "Inside," I urged Harvey, Wane, Emlyn, and Kai, scanning the street on which our safe house sat in Edinburgh. "*Quickly.*"

The second the door shut, I exhaled a rough breath, relieved to find my shields still intact even though I'd died. Most of them were built from relics I'd gathered over the years like the bone comb I stole from Halwen.

Halwen ... she was so still and pale, her body cold in Emlyn's arms. Her eyelids were closed now, but I couldn't purge the sight of her empty, staring eyes from my memory. My hands trembled when I pressed them flat to the door, pulling up a bright beam of power—and hissing when my magic sputtered, slashing pain through my chest.

Fuck. *Fuck.* A few jumps to a portal, and I was already drained. Persephone warned me it would take weeks to recover most of my strength and *months* before I was back at full power, but this was pathetic.

"Wane," I called, jogging up the stairs and biting back my pride. It tasted bitter. Poisonous. "Can you shield the house?"

A furrow formed between his dark brows when he turned to me, no suspicion in his eyes when he looked at me unlike at the Damned House. "I thought this house was warded."

"It is," I replied begrudgingly, trying not to stare at the blood dripping from his back onto the carpet at the top of the first flight of stairs. He was always bleeding; it never stopped. "But I want it armed to the teeth and it turns out being unmade plays havoc with a man's magic."

Wane just nodded, and shadows darker than any I'd ever seen gathered around him. Was I delirious, or was his magic blacker than even Cronus's?

I frowned even as relief loosened a knot in my chest when his magic spread out to cover the whole house. I couldn't help but remember the giant, void-dark form Cronus took in Olympus. I'd seen him enormous twice before but never made of pure black magic. Was that darkness of Cronus's making? Or was it stolen?

I knew how he worked, knew his obsessions. I'd heard of him trying to break his favourite pet for decades, trying to steal his magic. Did he succeed?

"Wane," I said haltingly, quietly, as the others rushed up to the second floor, eyes on Haley in Emlyn's arms.

Wane paused, shoulders hunching around his neck. "The house is covered."

"I know," I said, jogging up to stand on the step below him. "Thank you. I—shit, I want to ask something that's probably traumatising, but tell me to fuck off and I will."

He stiffened, rising to his full height. He stared me down, stony and defiant. "Ask it."

"When Cronus—had you locked up." *Tortured you*, I'd almost said. "Did he take any of your magic?"

Shadows bound around Wane's shoulders, wrapping around his arms, his stomach, a protective veil. But he stared me straight in the eyes and said, "He tried for years, and I managed to hold out. Do *not* repeat this."

He waited for me to nod until he continued.

"When I felt Haley for the first time in a century, it gave me mental strength but—"

"It fucked with you physically," I guessed, my stomach sinking. She could never find out.

Anger slammed his brows down over his churning eyes. "He took advantage of me when my strength wavered—him and Andryas fucking Revairs."

"That snivelling little rat," I hissed, my face twisting into a sneer. "I almost killed him once. He's only alive because Cronus intervened."

Wane's anger cut through with satisfaction. He smirked. "I did, too."

"Shame the fucker's still alive," I said genuinely. "So, he managed to get some of your shadows. And now Cronus has them." The muscle flickering Wane's jaw was confirmation. "Can you sense them? Even when he has them? Did you sense them on Olympus?"

Wane shook his head, his stare snapping up when something shattered upstairs. Kai's snarl followed, Emlyn's growl matching it. How long had it been since Haley died? Twenty minutes? Thirty?

I grabbed Wane's shadow-wrapped shoulder and squeezed, braced for him to slam a fist into my stomach and surprised when he didn't. "Cronus will suffer for everything he's done."

Wane laughed bitterly, turning away from me and taking the stairs two at a time. "Does it even matter when Haley's gone?"

"Yes," I answered fiercely, wrath pouring through my chest, roiling in my stomach like acid. "He doesn't get to torture, manipulate, scar, and kill, and get away with it."

"Shut the fuck up!" Kai screamed down the hallway, louder when we reached the second floor landing.

Wane shook his dark head, giving me a pitying look. "He already has. He's the king of the gods and my mate is dead."

"So was I," I reminded him, stalking down the hallway to the bedroom the guys had gathered in. My heart stuttered at the sight of Halwen on the bed, her arms at her sides and her face turned to the ceiling, eyes closed. All she was missing was the coffin.

Fuck. My hands shook even though I knew what was in my pocket.

"No!" Kai exploded, hurtling himself at me like a bullet when I entered the room. I didn't take my eyes off my mate to defend myself, and I was emptied of power anyway; I had nothing to counter the army of snakes Kai unleashed at me.

"Kai!" Wane snapped, his face hard as he slashed his arm through the air. A dark, still wall of shadows slammed from ceiling to carpet in front of me, blocking Kai's venomous magic.

"I'm sorry, Kai," Wane added, and flicked his fingers. A rope of darkness coiled rapidly around Malakai, too fast for him to escape as it bound his arms to his sides. He hissed and snapped, pure murder on his face, but he couldn't reach me.

"What did you mean?" Wane asked urgently, giving Harvey and Em a meaningful look before he faced me. "You said *so was I.* What did you mean? You can bring her back the same way you returned?"

"No," I disagreed, keeping an eye on the feral men in the room as I crept closer to the bed, a stake stabbing me right in the heart at the sight of Halwen's still body. "For some reason, the queen of Hell decided I needed to be saved."

"That's where she went," Emlyn said hoarsely. He looked like shit, like a ghost. I probably did, too. "That day Haley ran away to Hell. The queen disappeared for something."

15

"If she brought you back, she could bring Haley back too," Harvey breathed, scrubbing his bronze face, hope bleeding into his eyes.

"She didn't," I said, swallowing hard as I perched on the bed beside my dead mate. It fucking *killed* me to see her like this. "Hades and Persephone are her in-laws, or at least something like that. They found my soul and did some weird mumbo jumbo death shit to give me a new body."

"So we find them," Wane decreed in that same hard voice. "We beg them to bring her back."

My hand refused to stay steady as I reached into my pocket and pulled out the tiny velvet box. What if it didn't work? What if the prophecy was wrong?

"Malakai, you incessantly demanded I tell you why I wanted a resurrection pearl," I breathed, my voice raw.

Kai sucked in a sharp breath, his eyes wide, all the violence draining from his expression until only the truth showed: devastation, grief, and brittle, aching desperation.

"It was part of why I obeyed Cronus no matter what," I told him, told all of them. I swallowed the lump in my throat and explained, "I'd pretty much had enough of my existence years ago. I pissed him off a few times just to see if he'd kill me, but I had a job to do, and he never let me forget it.

"Anyway," I added, clearing my throat. They didn't need my whole life story. "I obeyed him without question because thirty or so years ago he had me check up on Phoebe, one of his prized pets. And by check up on I mean threaten and terrify so she wouldn't dare to disobey him."

I waited for their disgust, but all I saw was desperation and confusion. "She's a titan, too, and the one who wrote the prophecy on Halwen's back. She told me some of what I already knew: Cronus had created me in part to be the mate of a woman called Halwen Vakhara and in part because I was to manipulate her into freeing him from his prison. She also

16

told me this complete stranger whose soul I'd been bound to would be the person my entire world revolved around. I laughed in her face. Well, the joke's on me," I added with a sad little laugh, reaching out to brush dirty pink hair out of Halwen's face. My stomach shrivelled at the cold temperature of her skin.

"She told me my mate would die," I said, finally getting to the relevant part. Harvey was utterly still beside me, not even his wings shifting. The others stared, waiting, silently pleading with their eyes. "And with her, all hope of there ever being a free world. Without her, we would be ruled by Cronus, but unlike the golden age of his first rule, this one would be tyrannical, and everyone would suffer. Surprising absolutely no one," I added dryly.

"She knew Haley would die," Emlyn said, his voice gravelly as he knelt on the other side of the bed, taking her cold hand in his. "What else?"

"She didn't tell me how she'd die or why, or even when, but she said I'd need a resurrection pearl if I stood any chance of bringing her back. I honestly could not have given two fucks at the time. I scared her like I was supposed to and went on with my life. You three were in Alphaven at that point, and you'd forgotten Halwen, which meant you weren't a threat to Cronus. He didn't even bother checking on you.

"I only remembered Phoebe's warning when I met Halwen, and she consumed every single thought I had. I told Cronus I'd stop 'acting out' as he called it, but only if he gave me a pearl."

Eyes burned the side of my face; I shot Kai a wary look, checking he was still tied by shadows. He had yet to speak but there was no shadow gagging him.

"Did he give it to you?" Wane rasped. "The resurrection pearl?"

"Cronus?" I scoffed. "No. The bastard led me on and

promised he'd give it to me when I delivered you all to the Damned House and fulfilled my task. I managed to convince him I wanted it to bring back my—your mother. I'd never met her, so it was easy to put on an act about wanting the mother I'd never had. He'd never have agreed to the bargain if he thought I'd use it on Halwen. He bought the lie, but mostly so he could keep me in line when I started prioritising Halwen over his commands. He never planned to give it to me."

I turned the velvet box over in my hand, stroking a knuckle down my cold mate's face. All their eyes zeroed on the box. "So I asked Hades and Persephone for one," I said casually, my swollen throat and tight voice somewhat undermining the flippant statement. "I told them Cronus would win unless they gave me one, and they didn't even hesitate. They want Cronus dead as badly as we do. They didn't even ask who it was for."

I snapped the box open, swallowing hard at the supernatural gleam on the lilac-silver pearl inside. Bodies pressed close behind me—my brothers, I thought. But were they really my brothers when I was made, not born, a creature ripped into existence from their sun and shadow? I wasn't their blood, wasn't even born, not the first time and not this second time either.

"It might not work," I forced past my swollen throat. "There's no guarantee."

"Do it," Kai said—not hissing but ... pleading. "Do it. Use it. *Please.*"

I met his eyes and saw my own panic and brokenness mirrored back to me. When you became obsessed with someone, you built your whole life around that person, and without them you were nothing. I was on autopilot, not really existing, the only thing keeping my heart beating and body moving the pearl in my hand. This single, fragile chance.

I plucked the pearl from its bed of silk, my fingers shaking hard now. *Fuck, don't you dare drop it. This is the only thing that's ever mattered in your whole life, the only good thing you've ever done, so don't you dare fuck this up, you piece of shit.*

The pearl hummed and tingled between my fingers, not entirely solid. I pressed it to Halwen's chest, my palm flat over the pearl, and held my breath as I stood. I only hesitated a split second before I drove my palm down on her chest, forcing the pearl inside her body. Barely breathing, I lifted my hand. The pearl was gone, its power absorbed by her body.

"Did it work?" Kai asked breathlessly, stumbling forward when Wane unbound his shadows. Kai threw himself at the bed, scanning Halwen's face as we all did, praying colour would return to her face, her eyelids would flutter, and she'd suck in a gasp.

"Please," Harvey whispered. *"Please."*

Five seconds passed.

Ten.

"Please," Harvey chanted, a litany of desperation that got raspier with every second. "Haley, *please.*"

I didn't take my eyes off her for a second, but my chest caved in when she didn't move even a millimetre.

Minutes passed and she stayed cold, still, and dead.

I ripped away from the bed, my fist pressed to my mouth as I fought to conceal the broken mess inside me. For a little while, I'd actually liked being alive, actually had something worth sticking around for, and now it was gone. She was gone.

I jumped when a heavy hand landed on my shoulder, and I looked at Emlyn with dead eyes when he squeezed it and said, "You tried. It could have saved her."

I tried, but it wasn't good enough. I was never fucking good enough.

CHAPTER 3

HALWEN

I like it here, I thought, stretching my arms out at my sides as I floated through a pool of soft darkness, like a calm ocean. I hadn't had a holiday in forever, but I deserved this one. Shame the sun blazing down on me was as dark as ink and just as warm.

This isn't a holiday, the grumpy voice of my new vacation bestie argued, appearing on the tiled floor outside the pool I floated in.

Everything was made of different shades of pitch, black, void, and sable, but I could make out the pool, the sun loungers, palm trees, and the cute little beach shack just fine. I wore a polka dot bikini that was definitely pink despite being varying shades of charcoal, and I'd put my hair up into cute braided pigtails.[1]

You're dead, he went on, ignoring my pouting scowl as he sat on the edge of the pool, his six-foot-five, rake-thin body dressed in a sharp suit and his shoes shiny and lacquered. His hair was equally shiny, slicked back from his hawkish face. His name was Erebus, but I'd been calling him Busty because he couldn't stop me.[2]

Don't be a killjoy, Busty.

But you are *dead. This is just an echo of your soul I was able to preserve because Cronus possesses a thread of my darkness.*

Boo, I replied, sticking out my tongue. *You're no fun. Go get me a mojito.*

I am Erebus, the true darkness, one of the first—

Beings to exist in the known universe, I cut in, sliding a pair of sunglasses over my eyes and deciding I'd rather be on an inflatable than floating on my back. *Yeah, you might have mentioned that.*

An inflatable appeared under me, made of pitch black shiny plastic in the shape of a dagger. Cute.

And still, you order me around like I'm a common god. Wouldn't you rather go back?

I frowned, kicking my feet through the calm water. *To what?*

Forgotten already? Busty sighed. *We just had this conversation. Your mates are waiting for you. They've gone to a lot of trouble to give you a second chance at life.*

Hm. I dipped my hand into the dark water, watching it play over my skin. *Good for them.*

Busty pinched the bridge of his sharp nose. *You have to go back.*

Don't.

Alright, he agreed. *Then Cronus wins.*

Rage flickered through me at that name, visible as veins of red lightning in my hands, but I couldn't remember why I was so furious at hearing it.

Better. Think of Cronus and how you're going to make him pay for hurting your mates. Remember them, Halwen. You need to remember them. They're your tether to life.

I rolled my eyes. *I'm staying with you. I like it here; it's calm. Quiet.*

Busty laughed, which wasn't a good omen. I slanted a suspicious look his way just before I was dumped off my inflatable. I yelped when water rushed over my head, except the water wasn't wet, it was a cloud of shadows and darkness and—

It spat me out in the middle of a chaotic crossroads. Inky traffic roared around me, chugging along every road and leaving dark trails of smoke so thick that I coughed.

Still peaceful? Erebus asked, materialising beside me. *Still want to stay?*

I glared at the tall bastard. *Give me back my pool.*

It was never yours and never a pool. It's merely your soul's impression on my darkness.

Yeah, well, give me my soul impression thing back, I huffed, crossing my arms over my chest and glaring when my bikini changed to leathers and heavy boots, twin daggers hanging at my hips. My eyes snagged on them, the wavy edges, the inscription down the centre of each blade, the hilts that were wrapped in grey fabric I somehow knew was baby pink. I blinked, and they were singed, blackened by—Cronus.

That bastard burned my knives, I hissed.

That bastard, Busty replied with thinly veiled rage, *stole one of your knives and now possesses a weapon never intended for him. One capable of slaying any god and dangerously wounding even a titan.* He glanced at me and waited until I met his eyes before he added, *You dangerously wounded him, even if he healed the cuts. The damage runs deep. There's an advantage you can press—his physical weakness—even if his power is vast enough to swallow the entire world.*

You're cheery, I said, deadpan, watching a glossy double

decker careen past us with a screech and up a curving grey road lined with elegant buildings and strung with flags. *Where are we?*

Piccadilly circus, he replied, *but before they put up those gods forsaken screens.*

I gave him a strange look.

He tilted his face up, his nose wrinkled in a sneer. *This place was sacred before it was ruined.*

Weren't most places? I joked, and set off walking up the strange, crescent moon street.

Busty followed, seeming sulky about it. *Olympus is sacred too,* he said, always nudging me back to talking about what happened before he brought me here. *Even if it was built on the site of the Titanomachy and all its bloodshed.*

I gave him a blank look.

The war of the titans, he tried, waiting for some spark of recognition. *The battle of the gods?* He sighed. *I can't tell if you never knew, you can't remember if you knew, or you're just being contrary.*

Probably all three, I quipped. *What's your point?*

Stop avoiding the matter at hand.

The matter at hand, I parroted. *You're so serious.*

I'm watching a war unfold in another dimension. Of course I'm serious. You might like it here in the darkness, but you can't stay. Besides, do you realise why these shadows are so reassuring to you?

Nope, I replied, following the curving road—and letting out a throaty sound when the road unmade itself around me, replaced with a forest wrapped around a big, rustic house.

Unmade... Why was that word familiar? Why did it fill me with grief and dread and endless, shattering pain?

I am Erebus—

I sighed, rolling my eyes. Erebus had a damn complex; he was obsessed with his titles.

The first darkness to grace the world, and the personification of true shadows from which the day and the aether were born.

I glanced at him, my smirk becoming a genuine smile. *You've got kids?*

Yes. And many descendants; my family is vast and spreads across all species and races. Most possess only a sliver of darkness, but there is one in whom darkness lives as strong as my own. Stronger, perhaps, for what it has endured.

You're talking in riddles, I pointed out, eyeing the two-storey house as we walked through a low-slung garden towards it. There was a vegetable patch on one side, rose bushes and other flowering plants on the other.

My heart twisted up tight and I stopped before I could reach the house, images overlapping. In one vision the house was burning, fire pouring through every room in a cruel flickering glow.

Remember, Busty said, his voice quieter, sadder. The dark wrapped around my shoulders like a hug, and a weight fell from me even as a lump swelled in my throat.

Oh, I murmured when he pulled me into an embrace, and I realised it wasn't the darkness hugging me but him. It felt like being held by my dad, the same care and protectiveness and worry, and my eyes stung.

My shadows are a comfort to you because Wane, your mate, inherited them from me. Both him and Harveil are descended from me, but the younger twin received my daughter's sunlight.

I blinked. I'd always thought Wane was the younger one.

Wait. Shit. He was making me remember, reminding me of a life I knew was full of pain and misery and torture. I didn't *want* to remember. But now he'd cracked the door open on my memories, they came pouring out until I couldn't look at the house without seeing it in flames.

This is mean, I said, my voice choked.

Erebus stroked my hair like I was a teenager sobbing because her first love had just broken up with her.[3]

They're waiting for you, Busty murmured, his shadows leeching all my bite and snarl until I wanted to sob. *You can't stay here, Halwen. It was always temporary. It's time to go back.*

Back to agony and crying and fighting for my life?

I've had enough, I told him. *I'm so fucking tired, and life sucks. I'm staying dead.*

Erebus moved back, his dark brow knotted and sympathy in his glossy black eyes. *Life isn't made of only bad, and equally death isn't only good. There's suffering in death, and peace in living. But,* he added pointedly, and I was already rolling my eyes, *your mates don't have much peace right now. Should I show you them?*

I turned away, a lump in my throat. The house drew my eye, as it always did, and a tight ache formed in my chest. My eyes burned. *Please don't.*

Oh, Halwen, he sighed, standing shoulder to shoulder with me now. *It's okay to be afraid. Every mortal being is afraid.* He glanced at me. *Some immortal beings, too, though they'd deny it.*

I swallowed hard, blinking a tear free. *What happens if I go back? How long before someone else kills me, or—*

Or kills one of my mates.

Oh gods, we were *killed.* Cassander Locke murdered us. Cronus murdered Wynvail. And Wane—Wane was tortured every day for a hundred years.

Show me what happened to Wane, I rasped, startling Erebus.

Halwen, no. Darkness surged against my shoulder, turning me away from the house, and it was so familiar that I couldn't breathe for a moment. These were Wane's shadows, the darkness I'd woken up wrapped in for ten years, the darkness that had shielded me, protected me, cared for me.

Show me.

It won't fix anything. It won't help you, Halwen. It will only make returning more painful.

I shrugged. *Then I won't return. Problem solved.*

But I was remembering more and more, remembering who I'd been in life, who I'd loved.

I remembered Kai stalking me when I snuck out of the safe house. He stopped me in the middle of the street with the night dark and close around us and presented me with the greatest gift I'd ever been given.

And Emlyn siting on the floor outside the bathroom for three hours when I miscarried for the second time, murmuring endless assurances that they still loved me, still wanted me, and this wasn't my fault.

Harvey almost melting a baking tray trying to make my favourite cake for my birthday, his chest covered in flour, batter all over his hands, and a look of pure and utter defeat on his face when he met my eyes. A lemon cake had sat, blackened, on the countertop. *I'm so sorry, Sugarplum, I fucked up. I wanted everything to be perfect, but—* I'd kissed him, so touched I'd almost cried.

Wane, my beautiful Wane, who fought back his panic and trauma just to touch me, kiss me, hold me, who was so thoughtful that he'd knew everything I needed before I even realised it, who cared so much and loved so hard that it should have been impossible. Wane, who refused to forget me even though Cronus tried *for a hundred years* to wipe me from his mind.

And Wynvail, who walked willingly into death just because it would make me happy, who gave up his own life to save Wane's because despite everything he'd endured, every evil thing he'd ever done, he was still *good.*

I blinked, and the house wavered around us, shadows rushing around it, swallowing it, and replacing it with—an endless black corridor, devoid of hope and light and mercy.

My breath choked off in my lungs.

I don't think this is a good idea, Erebus muttered, *but I'll honour your request.*

I swallowed hard, the walls pressing in on me, the stagnant scent of old blood and damp heavy in my lungs. Wane had lived here for a hundred years. I could bear it, too.

CHAPTER 4

EMLYN

I wasn't allowed to fall apart. Too many people were relying on me for me to slip. Without me keeping them together, taking care of them, keeping them alive, what would happen?

Kai had fallen into a silent, empty shell, staring into space and not speaking to anyone. It was a thousand times worse than any fists thrown through the wall, worse than yelling so loud it shook the whole house.

Harvey had locked himself in one of the bathrooms and hadn't come out in hours.

Wane wasn't locked away, and wasn't folded up, hidden by shadows, in the corner either. But darkness clung to his body, and there was something dull behind his silver eyes. Something scarily dead. He walked from room to room like a zombie, never leaving Haley's side for long.

Wynvail was the worst. He wouldn't stand still for a second, running from room to room, floor to floor, grabbing books he swore would save Haley, unearthing magical object after magical object, leaving to make a deal with an old friend for a potion he promised could revive the dead. I wanted to slap him, to scream that she was dead and she was never coming back. She stabbed herself, she left us—

I sucked in a sharp breath, clenching my hands into fists as I rode out the pain. She left us, and I didn't know why she didn't fight. She could have stabbed Cronus, but she turned her dagger on herself.

I exhaled slowly, my shoulders shaking as I stood in the middle of the kitchen, not sure if I was supposed to be making coffee or food. Fuck.

I grabbed the edge of the island and bowed over it, my eyes burning, my throat closed tight. I saw that moment over and over, Haley driving the dagger into her stomach, red light erupting, Cronus tearing the knife from her and tossing her aside like she was trash. It was all I could see when I closed my eyes, not even the sight of her corpse laying in the bedroom erasing it. The corpse. My mate.

My mate was dead.

A broken breath shook my shoulders, but I choked out a curse and pulled myself upright, scrubbed my face, and wrestled my breathing under control. It took five minutes, but I composed myself and swallowed down my pain. I *had* to keep my shit together or I'd lose the rest of my family. Hales would be furious if they got hurt, and I'd rather die than do that to her.

"I'll take care of them," I rasped, curling my hands into fists when they shook, threatening to undo my composure again. "I promise, Hales. I'll make sure everyone's okay. I won't let you down."

Tea. That's what I was doing. Kai wouldn't eat, and I couldn't get through the bolted bathroom door to Harvey, but the others would drink tea if I left it for them. And maybe Harvey would finally unlock the door.

So I choked back the howl of devastation in my throat and made tea.

"You're sure you'll be okay?" I asked Wane, my heart aching as I watched him fold his knees up to his chest on the sofa, the position surely uncomfortable.

"I'll be fine," he replied robotically.

Indecision made me freeze, but I made Haley a promise and I wasn't about to break it. I crossed the room and kissed the top of Wane's head, then forced myself to walk away.

There was a portal halfway across Edinburgh that fed into Hell, heavily guarded on the other side but open on this end. I barely felt the cold rain pelt me as I approached the portal, the magic invisible except for a glimmer in the air. Security had been tightened since the Battle of Prague—AKA the war of angels and demons. The appearance of each rift was changed to make them harder to find unless you were a demon and felt the sizzling thrum of its power.

I didn't hesitate; I plunged right into its crackling power and clenched my jaw as it spat me out in the middle of a muddy field in Hell, too close to the Forest of Halwen for me to think of anything but my mate.

"State your name and purpose," a guard barked with zero originality.

I braced my hands on my knees as I caught my breath, swaying, the effects of the portal brutal.

"Emlyn Johahn. I'm here to visit family in the capital."

To pick up a family member, actually, but he didn't need to know that. I'd left Verena here and raced to save Halwen, but instead of saving my mate I witnessed her death. It didn't sit right with me that Verena was in the palace alone. If I'd been smarter, if I hadn't been so wrecked, I'd have kept the pen and appeared right in the heart of the palace. I didn't even know what happened to it. My mate died and the whole world fell apart.

"The capital's out of bounds," another guard replied, deep and disapproving. "Iarlon is unstable. There are too many riots; no one is allowed in."

My breathing slowed, nostrils flaring. I straightened slowly, magic building in my veins, filling every part of me. Blood buzzed in my ears like a swarm of bees.

I'd left Verena in a city now torn apart by violence.

"I'm sorry," the first guard said—a lanky blonde man with a thick moustache. "I'm going to have to ask you to return to Earth."

I blinked. Inhaled slowly. Counted. There were six guards, all armed, all powerfully built except for the lanky blonde.

"Are you deaf? Return to Earth," another guard barked, stepping forward—and screaming when emerald power blasted from me, eviscerating him.

He collapsed into five pieces, cut at perfectly straight angles, blood and gore on full display. I'd never liked it when people said *are you deaf?* in that tone.

I turned to the next guard when he came at me, and the next, and the next. All of them fell at my feet in dismembered limbs, their eyes staring as hollowly as Wane's had earlier, faces sliced in pieces.

Blood was deafening as it thundered in my ears, my chest rising and falling fast. The world had slowed, frozen with fury and screaming, bleeding grief.

The last guard ran, but I roared, and magic blasted from me like an earthquake, severing everything it met: the guard, the fence around the portal site, and deep into the trees around it. Trunks fell apart and crashed to the ground, a guard house sliced in five pieces to my left.

Within minutes, I stood in the middle of pure destruction, and I should have been horrified by it, but all I wanted to do was collapse to my knees and scream my grief to the red sky.

The red sky...

There's no loophole to exploit; you'll definitely kill them when the moon above Hell burns red.

That's what Oren told us before he inked beautiful flowers and ominous skulls on my mate's body. He was right. We *were* dead. We might have breathed, our hearts might have beat, but there was no life left in us.

The only thing driving me was grief and honour. I promised Hales to keep Verena safe, and I wasn't about to break that promise.

So I sucked in a rough breath and strode through the destruction. Towards a capital overrun with riots. I hoped more people got between me and Verena. I had more violence, rage, and magic to unleash.

I was nowhere near finished.

CHAPTER 5

I clenched my fist around the blood-slick handle of a mace I'd stolen from a woman I killed minutes or hours back, and grunt forced past my lips when I ripped it out of the shoulder of the latest bastard to charge at me. This one was pale-eyed, pink skinned, and naked like a mole rat. He also seemed to think he was strong and sensible enough to take Lucifer's place as the king of Hell. Most people rioting in Iarlon believed they were, too. I happily hacked my way through them, forcing my way closer to the palace at the top of the city, leaving a slew of bodies and gore behind me.

At some point, I picked up four devil's guards fighting their way through the streets, and either they recognised me on sight or were just glad of an additional soldier because they stuck at my back while I tore bodies apart and strode through the innards.

Hot blood covered me, soaked through my clothes, and even sloshed in my boots. I knew I was injured, too, but the only thing that mattered was the promise I made to my mate and the kid I had abandoned in the palace.

I didn't stop fighting until I'd hewn my way through the

crowd on the blood-soaked palace steps and through the towering door. My guard allies gave me a wide berth when I sliced the three men on the doors into pieces. It didn't matter how many people barred me from entering, I would get inside this palace and find Verena.

It was the only thing that mattered now. I bared my teeth when a new batch of guards rushed me, trying to shove me back out the door, but I grabbed another handful of magic and—

"Stop!" a hoarse voice commanded.

This batch of guards stepped back instantly, weapons and magic pointed away from me.

I clenched an inner fist around my own power. I'd only kill them if they got between me and my goal. I wouldn't needlessly slaughter, even if it was a much needed outlet for my pain and rage. For a moment as I fought, there was nothing else in the world except the razor edge of life and death. No loss, no mate lying cold in a bed in a safe house, no titan taking over the world with her stolen dagger.

"Emlyn," a tall, blonde man in his late thirties said, striding forward dressed in heavy leathers. A sword hung at his hip, but power radiated from him in its own threat. I recognised him. He was one of Hell's power players and the man who gave Haley the Alphaven mission. Cerny. I'd never heard anyone give him a surname.

"Shit, what happened to you?" he breathed, staring at the blood I was bathed in.

"He butchered his way through the whole city," a devil's guard offered behind me, giving me a wide berth since I killed the guards on the door. "He took out more rioters than the rest of us combined."

Cerny sucked in a surprised breath. "How bad is it out there?"

"Bad," I said flatly. "There's a girl here. Verena. I need to find her."

He straightened, eyes narrowed with warning and—pain. Deep, gnawing pain, the kind that scarred minds and left its mark. The kind that was leaving its mark on me right now. Who had he lost in the fight at Olympus?

"I won't let you harm a child."

I snapped my eyes up to his, rage pouring a growl from my throat, shaking my chest. The guards ducked around me and swiftly down the hallway.

"She's ours. I've come to take her home."

Cerny watched me suspiciously until I strode forward, inclined to kill him if it got me to Verena faster.

"Alright, I'll take you to her," he relented, turning to address the line of guards blocking the door. No one was currently trying to ram the door from outside, but how long before more rioters replaced those I'd killed, eager to try their hand at ruling? It was a fatal flaw of all demons; we wanted power. Some wanted magical power, others wanted riches and status, some wanted the power in freedom, but most wanted to rule, to stand over everyone else and be worshipped like a god. Kai and Harvey would accept the position in a heartbeat.

He angled his head as the guards let us through, and I followed quickly, silence loud in my head. "We found her a few hours ago, hiding out in one of the bedrooms. She nearly burned Russ when he coaxed her out. Her power is untested, but it's dangerously powerful."

I'd only seen sparks of golden light from her, but it wouldn't surprise me. She was a descendant of gods and still so young; she had a whole life to uncover vast scores of power. I'd make damn sure of it.

Which meant … I had to stay alive. For Verena. For the

promise I made Haley. As much as I didn't see the appeal in a world without her, I wouldn't leave her last wish unfulfilled.

"She won't tell us her name, but there's no other girl you could be looking for. Actually, that's not true; she told us her name is *go fuck yourself.*"

I tried to laugh, but it wouldn't form. My chest was empty.

"Cerny," a stern middle-aged woman called, racing to catch up to us. "They've broken through the east wing. We're trying to push them out and patch up the wall, but there are so many of them."

"Fuck," Cerny breathed, and there was no hiding the exhaustion in that sound. His gaze flicked between the woman and me, and he groaned. "If I find out you've kidnapped this girl, you'll be hunted to the ends of every realm. But go straight ahead and it's the third door on your left. Leahan, show me where they broke through."

Straight ahead, third door on the left. I didn't blink when Cerny ran off to deal with the rebels rampaging through the palace; I picked up my pace until I was running, my breaths coming in ragged scrapes, my head full of woolly silence.

I barely even noticed when the palace rocked with an explosion; I was already shaking on the outside, but horribly still inside. I threw open the third door, scanning the small armoury in a millisecond, my eyes landing on the slim teenage girl standing alone in the middle of the room, her body dripping steel and two wicked kindjal already arcing through the air towards me.

My shoulders slumped, casting off an enormous weight, and I heaved a sigh, knocking her clumsy blow aside as gently as I could while avoiding being speared like a pig.

"Are you hurt?" I demanded, peering down at Verena, scanning her for injuries and harm and shaking at the mere thought of it. She was angry but looked the same as when I left her, small and red-haired and covered in ash. "Did anyone bother you while I was gone? Give me their names and they're dead."

"What took you so fucking long?" she demanded, dropping her blades by her sides. "It's been a whole fucking day! You said *hours*."

I swallowed, my throat tight. "I'm sorry," I said gravely.

Verena scoffed, turning from me and sheathing her kindjal so she could grab more weapons off the walls—five small throwing stars, a little blade meant for close, tortuous work, and a sword far too heavy for her. "Whatever. What happened to you anyway?"

I stared at the gore covering me, the puddle of blood on the flagstones under me. "People got in my way. I told you I'd be back, and I wasn't about to break my word."

Verena lifted her messy red head, her eyes narrowed but surprise in the softness of her face. "Oh."

"Are you hurt?" I asked again, holding her gaze, blood roaring in my ears.

"No." She put the throwing stars in the pocket of a hoodie she'd got from gods knew where, and my heart skipped. Didn't she realise how easily they could slice through fabric and into her stomach? She could bleed out. She could be sliced apart like—like my Hales. "I'm fine. No one's tried to hurt me or even kick me out. There was this self-righteous blonde guy who tried to help me, but that's all. Everyone's too worried about the attacks to bother with me."

"Good," I grunted, scanning the walls and tables until I found a small leather pouch on a strap. I snatched it off the table and snapped open the closing. "Put the stars in here."

She eyed me warily but did as I ordered and accepted the pouch in her freckled hand with a strange expression. "Where are the others?"

"At a safe house on Earth. That's where I'm taking you."

"Why?" She crossed her arms over her chest, weapons clanking. "I'm nothing to you, why do you give a shit?"

My throat bobbed. I didn't know how to explain it.

"You remind me of my mate, and you were there in Aphrodite's cells with us. You're one of us now. We're all—we have nothing except each other, but we're family. Hales, she —she wanted to bring you home with us the second she heard you have no family. She grew up in care, too, and she—"

Fuck. My voice collapsed, choking off in my throat.

Keep it together, Emlyn. You can't break now; you can't break ever. *There are too many people relying on you—*

"What happened?" Verena asked, her tone completely changed and her green eyes wide as she stepped closer. "When you went back to Olympus. What happened?"

I dragged my teeth over my bottom lip, fighting back every ounce of emotion. I needed to be cold, to be in control, not the bloodied carrion of grief.

"Cronus won," I answered finally, my voice choked and deep.

We both flinched when another explosion rocked the palace, unsettlingly close. The rebels were going to bring the whole thing down. Was that what they wanted? Wipe out all traces of Lucifer and build a new palace on its grave?

The man hadn't been dead a day. Vultures, the whole fucking lot of them.

"We need to leave," I said, clearing my throat.

Verena's freckled face was pale, her features drawn. "They're going to get in, aren't they?"

"Yes."

She came closer to me, her thumb brushing the handle of a kindjal, over and over. "Is Cronus taking over Hell, too?"

"No. This is demons, circling the bloodied body of a wounded animal."

"That's graphic," she muttered, her posture stiffening further. "Why are they doing this?"

"Cronus devoured Lucifer. Hell is without a ruler." I reached out and took the heavy sword from her, holding it in one hand, my mace in the other. "They'll try to kill the queen and steal the title for themselves. Demons are ruthless animals, and Hell was at war only months ago. The realm's too unstable for something as big as this."

"Shit," Verena whispered, her eyes wide like a doll's. "How do we get out?"

I didn't know. That was the issue.

"Just follow me," I said after a too-long pause. "And stay close. If you get hurt, Hales will—"

Kill me. Except she wouldn't, because she was dead.

"I'll stay close," Verena promised, her voice careful and soft, like she was speaking to a spooked horse. Like she—like she knew. Or had guessed the truth at least.

I turned back to the door, gripping the weapons so hard my knuckles popped and—I staggered back from the door when a stampede of spirits hissed past, so thick that I couldn't see through them. *Fuck*, how many of them were there? A hundred? Five hundred?

I remembered the spirits Lucifer called on to fight Cronus and a knot unravelled in my chest. Backup—and a distraction for the rioters. Thank fuck. We could use this to—

Screaming began, so loud and guttural that I flinched back into the armoury and hastily shut the door. Wood wouldn't keep out an incorporeal spirit, but I felt better with it closed regardless.

"Emlyn?" Verena breathed.

"Shh," I whispered, not wanting to attract the army of spirits in the hall.

Guttural screams tore through the palace in a rippling wave; the spectres were undeniably attacking the palace's occupants. Torturing them by the sounds of it. They weren't even remotely on our side.

And how the fuck were we supposed to fight spirits? In all the books I'd read, there were only stories of vengeful spirits getting their revenge, never anyone *surviving* their wrath.

"Emlyn," Verena repeated in a squeak.

I spun—and my heart skipped.

Rage slowed everything, my numb soul freezing completely. A male spirit with short hair, square glasses, and psychopath eyes had his arm around Verena's throat. His lips were against her ear, and I couldn't hear what he told her, but all the colour bleached from her face.

"Magic," I ordered, my voice harsh when I locked eyes with her. "Now. I've got you, Verena."

She inhaled a shuddering breath. "I don't know how. I'm sorry, I can't, I don't know—"

Her gasping, panicked breaths threw petrol on the fire of my rage, and my lips peeled back from my teeth as I launched at the spirit. I plunged my mace into its cold body, but my hand and arm sank through his icy body too and I had to swerve to keep my balance. The impact I was used to never came, my weapon useless.

"That tickles," he laughed, a wide smile crossing his eerily transparent face. I could see the weapons on the wall through his silvery skin, and if I hadn't been so furious, that would have sent a chill through me.

"You don't get to touch my family," I growled, driving Verena's sword down through his shoulder, mindful of hurting her. The ghost didn't flinch, but I got close enough to knock Verena away from him.

She skidded across the room with a whimper she tried to suppress. My rage spiked higher, a constant snarl in my throat now.

"Shit," she gasped, the sound close to a sob. "Emlyn, there's more of them. They're everywhere."

"Get here," I ordered her, shaking all over, completely cold inside as I glared at the psycho ghost. "Put your back to my back. Don't move away from me."

Verena rushed to follow my instructions, her warm body shaking when she pressed against me. "What are we gonna do?"

"Fight like hell," I bit out.

There was nothing else we could do.

I reached for my magic and slashed the sword at the same time I let out a devastating arc of power, severing tables, gouging through the walls until there were deep slices cut in them. And yet the ghost stood unhurt, smiling, in front of me, with dangerous plans gleaming in his eyes. My family might be criminals and killers but there were lines we wouldn't cross, and I knew this ghost would. There was a reason the worst humans were sent to Hell to suffer for eternity.

If the worst of humanity had escaped their confinement into the boundaries of Hell proper, we were all screwed. Spirits were undefeatable. *Nothing* could kill a ghost. And even as I slashed more emerald magic through the room, more ghosts bled through the walls with hungry looks on their faces. They weren't looking at me; they looked past me to where Verena was shaking, the tips of her fingers sparking.

"I won't let them hurt you," I vowed. She was mine to protect, my fucking family. If Haley wanted to keep her, she was ours, no questions asked.

Fuck. *Hales.* My breathing hitched. I grunted when a ghost grabbed my wrist, ice biting into my skin, so suddenly painful that my knees weakened.

"Back off," Verena hissed, but her voice wavered.

I sent out another bright lash of magic, grasping for my

shifting magic. Another ghost grabbed me, so cold and painful that I couldn't concentrate, and I swore.

"Emlyn," Verena gasped. "I don't think I can—"

I spun, swallowing a snarl when cold hands grabbed at me, sinking into my back, and I caught Verena when her knees buckled. The look on her face was fierce, her teeth gritted and eyes furious, but the sparks at her fingertips died and she staggered into my arms with a gasp. The fact that she let me close said how weak and afraid she was. In full health, she'd have stabbed me.

She was so much like Haley, it hurt. She could have been our daughter.

"I've got you," I promised, dropping the axe so I could hold her up. "I'm right here, kid."

I wasn't going anywhere, even as more ghosts poured in. The whole palace had to be swarming with them by now. We were all going to die, weren't we? Not even Cronus could be blamed for this; it was demon greed, through and through.

I'm sorry, Haley.

It wasn't enough. No matter how hard I fought, cold bled into my bones, making me heavy, sluggish. My magic resisted as I tore it up through my body and shattered the room with it, tables left in ruins, even swords severed. But the spirits didn't avoid the magic in fear; they floated *towards* it, eager, hungry. I hissed when I felt their freezing touch on my power.

"Come here," I grunted to Verena, pulling her stiff body closer and snapping my wings out around her. It was better the spirits touched me, weakened me. Maybe Verena would stand a chance of getting out of here.

"What are you doing?" she demanded weakly. "Don't be fucking—stupid..."

She was weak. *Oh, gods.* My stomach dropped. I'd come to save her from an unstable city, but there was nothing I could do against *spirits,* and now her life was being sucked out of her.

The first spirit chuckled, his laugh louder than before and his eyes sharper, clearer behind his glasses. Actually, his whole body was clearer. More solid. Motherfucker just stole our lifeforce.

I growled, the only thing I could do when my arms were trapped by my wings around Verena. I wanted to shred the bastard into ribbons, and now that he was more solid, I might be able to harm him. Maybe. It was a fool's chance, but if it wouldn't have left Verena unprotected, I would have taken it.

But Haley had claimed her, and she was one of us—alone, mistreated, and raging at the world because of it. She was exactly like Harvey or Kai, exactly like me. And no way in any goddamn realm in the universe was I leaving a thirteen-year-old kid unprotected. So I just snarled my threats and kept her bound up in my wings, my growl sinking deeper when cold hands plunged into my body, leeching all warmth, stealing my energy.

The queen was powerful enough to take on gods and win, and her inner circle had been right there with her. They killed *Zeus.* They could figure out how to contain an army of murderous spirits; I just had to hold on long enough for … long enough for … for…

"Emlyn?" Verena asked shrilly. "Hey? Don't go to sleep. Please don't go to sleep."

"Won't," I vowed, but my tongue was thick and cold in my mouth and my body stooped, so much heavier than before.

"Shit," she breathed. "Hey! Back the fuck up, leave us alone. I'm warning you."

I was too weak to do anything when she shoved my right wing down and threw her hand up, golden light flaring at her fingertips. Even with my eyes slipping shut, I knew it wasn't enough magic to frighten a spirit, let alone the thirty who'd invaded the weapons room.

I braced myself for a slow, painful death and recoiled in surprise when light erupted in front of us, so powerful that all the spirits flocked towards it like moths to flame. She did it. Verena had saved us. She—

"What the fuck is taking so long?" a hateful, so fucking *welcome* voice snapped.

The beam of light split as Wynvail stepped out of it. He scanned the two of us and straightened, stalking over to us like a vengeful god.

Spirits scattered, but not out of fear; they rushed to where remnants of his moon-bright light remained, vultures through and through.

"Jesus," Wynvail breathed. "You don't look so good, Emlyn."

"The ghosts attacked us," Verena said urgently, her slim arm banding across my back like she could support me despite being a fifth of my size. "They came through the fucking walls."

"Ghosts will do that," Wynvail said dryly, but without any true amusement. More like he was going through the motions of humour. "Ready to get out of here?"

"Fuck yes," Verena breathed.

But she flinched into me when the psycho spirit rushed at us. "You think you can escape? I can taste your magic, little lamb. It's *delicious.*"

A weak growl shook my throat. I forced my eyes open further, grabbing Verena's arm and pulling her closer, forgetting to be gentle. I'd apologise later when we were safe.

Wynvail wrapped his hand in silver-white light and punched the spirit in the throat. He staggered back, rage in his milky eyes, but Wynvail was already turning to us, grabbing my shoulder and Verena's arm.

White light enveloped us, stealing us away before the

spirits could leech any more of our power. I was so fucking glad Wynvail was alive again. He was a smug, cruel bastard and I hated him but ... he was family. He was one of us, too.

And he just saved our lives. Saved my promise.

The light relinquished its grip on us, and I fell to my knees on the thick rug in the safe house living room, panting, my head spinning and my whole body weak. I was surprised to hear multiple voices crying out, and even more surprised when I lifted my heavy head and found everyone here—Wane, Harvey, and Kai, all rushing towards me.

I must have been in Hell longer than I realised. I didn't expect my absence to be noticed, let alone for it to cause the panic I saw in their eyes.

I was so used to staying strong, beating back any emotion that might interfere with taking care of my family, that my eyes stung when they all fussed over me, snapping questions —Kai—offering soft reassurances—Wane—and slamming healing power into my body until my back arched and I howled in pain—Harvey.

When the fire-hot magic stopped punishing my insides, I panted, leaning into Harvey as my head spun and settled.

"Thank you."

He knocked his head into mine. "Any time. What the fuck happened?"

"Hell is falling apart," I replied, catching my breath. "Riots, rebels, spirits everywhere."

"Hell is *falling* more like," Wynvail muttered, stalking over to give me a once-over. "Still alive then?"

"For now," I replied dryly, earning a surprising smile. I wasn't sure he'd ever smiled at me so genuinely before. It was strange.

"She's ... she's not here, is she?" Verena said, making us all jump.

She stood exactly where we'd landed when Wynvail transported us. Her arms were wrapped around herself, and she stared at the room with eyes bright with pain. She looked so young, so afraid.

"Haley's ... gone?" She swallowed and looked at us—at Wane and I, the ones who were locked up beside her in that awful place. When I nodded, Verena clenched her jaw and glanced away. "Fuck! Fucking shrivel-dicked motherfucking *fuck.*"

Watching her scrub her face with hands still ashen from Olympus hurt. I lumbered to my feet, unsteady even though Harvey had healed the spirits' damage.

Verena's throat bobbed. "This isn't fucking fair. It's not *right.* If you'd stayed with her, if you hadn't wasted time getting me out of Olympus—"

"No," Kai cut in, his voice hard enough to make her flinch. Shit. "That wasn't wasted time. You're family, Verena. Like Em said before, we're keeping you."

He strode across the rug, beating me to her, and yanked her into a rough hug. "Don't do this blame bullshit. None of what happened was your fault.

"I'm so sorry," she breathed, her voice tight with emotion.

A pit opened in my stomach as I stood beside them and realised we didn't just have to keep Verena safe from Cronus or spirits or fuck knows what else. We had to look after her, *raise* her. She was ours, really ours. But I didn't know how to do this without Haley.

I'd dreamt of children for a hundred years, pictured my life full of their laughter and chaos. Every time we conceived it was the greatest fucking gift. Every time we lost the baby, it felt like I'd been stabbed in my heart. But every time, I imagined children *with our mate.* Never just *us.* How could five grief-stricken bastards raise a teenage girl?

We were going to fuck this up.

46

But she didn't have anyone else. And I meant what I said. We were keeping her.

I didn't know what to say to make her feel better, but I overlapped my arms with Kai's and held them both, feeling like I'd been kicked in the stomach when the brothers did the same, all of us clutching tight, a mess of grief and shock.

"We're getting revenge, right?" Verena asked tentatively. "We're avenging her death. Right?"

"Right," Kai agreed fiercely.

We couldn't. Not when Verena was relying on us. I knew that would be an argument, knew it would split our family, but I didn't have the energy to argue right now.

So I said nothing at all.

CHAPTER 6

HALWEN

I forced myself to walk, my eyes glancing off closed doors, searching for the open one, the one that led to my mate.

This way, Busty said, giving me an assessing look. He clasped my elbow and guided me into the narrow maw of a pitch-black tunnel, so silent that our breaths and footsteps were the only noise echoing off the curved stone walls.

Where are we going? I whispered, only his hand on my elbow keeping me grounded as fear beat at my chest. All the hairs rose down my arms, and I knew I didn't actually have a body here, I was only a soul, but it certainly felt like I did as a chill sank into my bones.

Cronus's throne room.

I inhaled a sharp breath. He had a throne room? Was that where he—where Wane—

This tunnel goes on for miles, Erebus said, a note of rage entering his cool voice. *It's designed for maximum fear, so his victims—or pets as he's so intent on calling them—will lose their courage and morale before they ever reach him.*

A question bit at my tongue, and I tried to swallow it back, but it had been screaming at me ever since we stepped into this place.

Why didn't you stop it?

Erebus's shadows seemed to darken until there was an even darker stain of blackness beside me, but I felt the rage pulsing from him, felt it bleed through his hand into my elbow.

Like all of the first beings, I can't influence anything that happens outside my domain. All I can do is observe. If I was able to touch the Earth, Hell, or Heaven, I would have smited that cruel excuse for a titan centuries ago. He might be the most powerful being alive, but if I could reach Olympus, he wouldn't stand a chance.

He paused. *Wane might achieve the same.*

I swallowed hard, the weight of darkness pressing around me, crushing the air from my chest, crawling up my spine like a fell insect, reminding me over and over that Wane had lived here for *a hundred years.*

I can't ask that of him.

He might want it, Busty countered. *He deserves revenge after all.*

I don't want him anywhere near this psycho, I snarled, turning to shove Busty away from me. *And you don't get to ask. He's been through enough.*

Have you so easily forgotten that he stood alongside you to fight Cronus?

I bared my teeth in his vague direction. *Have you so easily forgotten that he was thrown so hard he was left unconscious?*

His heartbeats are full of rage and blood, Halwen. Don't deny him what he might need.

My nostrils flared. I said nothing as I turned away and

stalked down the pitch tunnel, wishing I could see my feet as I placed them on the ground, wishing I could smell anything other than blood.

Wait, Erebus said, catching my arm. *Before you enter, I should warn you—*

But I powered ahead, and only grounded to a halt when I flew through a door—or walked through the wall, I couldn't fucking see—into a tall marble room lit in shades of muted grey.

It was completely empty except for the great and hideous throne made of black stone, carved with screaming faces and scenes of violence—and the man kneeling before it, black wings slumped on the cold floor and his head bowed, his bare back rising and falling with rapid breaths.

I blinked and the throne was no longer empty; Cronus sat there, lounging casually with a gleam in his eye that promised another torturous scene to add to his throne.

Halwen, Erebus said in a tight voice. *You need to prepare yourself for—*

But Cronus leant forward in his throne and a third man appeared from the darkness, dark-skinned and tight-eyed, his movements stiff like he was hiding an injury. This man—immortal but not godly—stood behind the kneeling figure, the figure I would recognise anywhere.

Don't fucking touch him, I snarled, and raced across the room, my footsteps echoing off the high marble ceilings. But when I grabbed the stranger's arm, my touch slid off him like he was made of light, and all I could do was stand there as Cronus ordered Wane to stay kneeling, using his oily, disgusting magic to force my mate still as—

Oh gods.

He knelt, unmoving, not struggling, as his wings were hacked messily and cruelly from his back. My own wings wrapped tight to my body, phantom pain chasing through them. I couldn't tear my eyes away. Wane didn't flinch, didn't even move until the heinous man stepped back, severed wings in his hand, and Cronus nodded.

Wane fell forward with a scream, his forehead pressed to the marble and his arms wrapped around his middle, the wounds on his back weeping violent blood. Even though it was grey in Erebus's vision, I saw red, saw it spill across his bronze back and bloom on the floor as he screamed until his voice broke and only hoarse, sobbing noises escaped his throat.

I knelt beside my mate, trying to hold him and snarling in frustration when my hands slid off his body.

This had happened. It wasn't happening right now, it was only a memory, but it had happened. This is what Cronus did to my mate. What that bastard holding Wane's wings did.

When I find you, I told the stranger in a voice colder than ice, *I'm going to make you wish you'd used that knife to cut your own throat.*

Wane is not here, Erebus said soothingly. *He's at your home, waiting for you. You need to go back Halwen.*

I swallowed hard. Your home... No, my home was burned to the ground. But the safe house, the house Wynvail painstakingly and thoughtfully made for me ... *was* it home?

You can't protect him while you stay here, Erebus went on, his voice low and soft.

But it was like a match struck against my rage and fear, and I jerked back, baring my teeth at him. *That's why you let me come here, why you showed me what Cronus did to Wane. So you could use it to manipulate me into leaving—*

Because you won't listen! he snapped, shadows flaring around him, swallowing every part of the room except Wane bleeding on the floor and Cronus smiling on his foul throne. *The entire world is at stake, your mates' lives are at stake, and* anyone else you love. Everyone will be enslaved or slaughtered—those are the only options.

And you think I can change that, I replied flatly.

There's an unbreakable prophecy that warns you will. It isn't a promise to those fighting Cronus; it's an omen for the titan himself. You can, and will kill him, Halwen. But not if you stubbornly cling to death. You should be alive, thriving, and murderous. So go!

I tried to kiss Wane's head, my throat tightening when he was like a ghost against my lips. I stood, glancing at Erebus, my friend nothing but a writhing mass of darkness in front of me, not even his body or features visible now.

Why do you care so much? You can't even touch the living world, in your own words, so why does it matter what happens to the rest of us?

The darkness ripped away until Erebus stood there, a thousand emotions churning in his black eyes. Wouldn't you care about your children and your children's children? Would death erase the love you felt? Would being locked away from the living stop you wanting them safe and cared for?

All my anger drained away, sympathy and pain tangling in my chest.

No, I admitted quietly, remembering the first impression I'd got of Erebus when he swept me away from the brutal site of my murder: safety and parental love. Sorry, I added, my shoulders slumping.

He came closer, his dark face softening. You might not be my child, Halwen, but your soul is entwined with the souls of my descendants, which makes you mine to protect. And letting you stay here isn't protecting you.

I couldn't look at Wane, bleeding and sobbing on the ground. Erebus swept his hand, and the ground was empty, the bastard who mutilated my mate erased too.

And yet Cronus remained on his vile throne, staring at his hand where—where shadows pooled in his palm. The shadows he stole from Wane. My heart skipped, rage filling my chest again.

I'm scared to go back, I admitted to Busty. *Living hurts, and mostly it fucking sucks. There's no pain here.*

Isn't there? he asked softly, guiding my face to the marble wall above Cronus's throne.

I froze, blood roaring in my ears. Two black wings were stretched wide on display, blood running down the pale stone from the places they'd been hacked off. Like Wane's wounds still bled even now, years upon years later.

I know it hurts you to see this, daughter, Erebus breathed, pressing his shoulders to mine, offering comfort in our shared pain. Had he watched it as it happened? Was this moment a replay of a scene in the mortal world—or was it *his* memory? How much did it kill Erebus to watch all this play out to his family and be unable to stop it?

Are you dead, or just trapped? I asked, slanting a look at him, my … friend? He wasn't really here, like I wasn't really here. This was just his magic letting us speak and share the same vision. I didn't know where he really was, or even where I was. Still on Olympus? Or did Cronus eat my dead body?

I'm not truly sure, he replied, his eyes fixed on the bleeding wings on the wall. *I've been here so long, I'm not sure I'd know how to be alive.*

So you don't want me to kick down the doors of your prison and get you out? I asked seriously.

His grim mouth flicked up in a shocking smile. I stared in unabashed surprise. *You know what I want, Halwen, and you know what you need to do.*

Kill Cronus, yeah, I knew. And … I was ready. To leave. To fight the bastard. To find a way to finally kill him. If some loony prophet said I could, who was I to argue? I was already dead; I might as well go back and risk my life, see if I couldn't take Cronus with me next time.

Cronus wants Wane's shadows, Busty said without prompting, *because it's original, true power in its rawest form. He could use it to unmake the whole world—and reshape it in his image.*

Shit, I breathed, trying to imagine what a world would look like ruled by Cronus. How many people would kneel, bleeding, before him? How many wings would be severed and displayed as an eternal taunt?

Wane could use it to the same end, Erebus added casually. *And so could any descendant.*

Wait, so all your children are running around with the ability to change the world? My eyes were wide, panic making my breathing fast. What if they were all insane? Would that be worse than Cronus's world?

That's not quite what I said, he replied with a mysterious smile.

He blinked and Cronus and the throne vanished, Wane's wings disappearing with him.

With all the love in my heart, I hope I never see you again, Halwen.

Rude. I narrowed my eyes, my heart aching. But panic struck as I felt myself fading, my limbs less solid. I couldn't feel my chest anymore. *What if I need to talk to you, or I need your help?*

Erebus smiled, a true, deep smile. *You have everything you needed from me. You're going to be just fine. You can find me in every shadow in every realm, but you won't hear my voice again. You won't see my face again.*

I shook my head, panic clawing through me. I couldn't feel my legs. Shit, did I even have legs?

What am I supposed to do? I don't know how to kill Cronus.

Use your power, Halwen. All of it, every kind that lives inside you. You have more than he could ever dream to possess, even devouring most of Olympus. You have true, unbridled power, untainted by misery and pain. That's more powerful than any god he's swallowed.

That makes no sense!

I tried to reach for him, but I didn't have hands. Oh fuck, I didn't have *hands.*

Trust yourself, and don't be afraid of your power. It won't hurt you; it will only do as you bid it. You have the strength to do this, I promise you. If you need advice, I believe the most appropriate counsel is a modern term: give 'em hell, Halwen.

What the fuck was I supposed to do with that?

I opened my mouth to demand an answer because there was no way he was leaving me with that and *only* that to help me kill a titan, but I no longer had a mouth and—

I sucked in a sharp breath, pain erupting through every part of my body.

Ugh, great. I was alive again.

And typical—everything hurt.

CHAPTER 7

*I*t was kinda rude that no one was sitting beside my deathbed when I woke, but that was fine. Totally fine. I wasn't insulted or hurt *at all.* My brows slammed down over my eyes and a scowl flattened my mouth, but that was completely unrelated.

I swung my legs out of bed—and inhaled a rapid hiss at the riot of aches and pains in my body. Shit, my stomach was tender.

Oh yeah, I stabbed myself. Fun times.

My fingernails pressed into the mattress as I sat there, panting and cursing Erebus for making me come back. But now I was here, in pain and pissed off as usual, now I was *alive* ... I was glad to be back.

Even if Cronus tried to eat me again, even if I had to stab myself again, I could see Wane smile that tentative smile of his, and see Kai flick his forked tongue out in a sulky hiss, and watch Harvey try to beat the world record for number of bread rolls he could balance on his head,[1] and soak up the simmering weight of Wynvail's obsessed stare, and feel the weight of Emlyn's body against mine, his arms wrapping me entirely until it felt like everything would be okay in the world.

Fuck, I needed a hug.

I set my feet on the ground, wincing at the icy flash of the floorboards, and stretched my toes out to the pink shag rug in the middle of the room.

"Okay, Haley," I breathed, psyching myself up. "Now all you have to do is stand up. Easy peasy, greasy beefy."[2]

I pushed up on one leg, and when nothing disastrous happened, I confidently rose on both legs—and hissed when my left knee tried to drop me on my ass. My wings snapped out on instinct, and I had to bite back a scream at the pain that erupted through cartilage and bone.

Cocksucking, motherfucking *owww.*

I panted, grabbing the bedframe and gripping it in white-knuckled fingers, but the longer I stood, the more willing my leg was to be a leg.

"Good leg," I praised it, as if my thigh might have a praise kink and strive to be its best self.[3]

I sucked up all my courage, ignored the flash of a vision I had of eating carpet when my leg collapsed, and took a step.

Hey, look at that, I was walking.

I was amazed when I reached the door, and even more so when I pulled it open and walked down the hall. Holy fuck, I was walking. I had legs, I wasn't dead, and I was *walking.*

Erebus was going to be so smug about this. He was right; I did need to come back. I was glad I hadn't stayed in the darkness, hiding from my problems.[4]

There was a patch of shadow behind a potted fern. I stopped my slow procession down the hallway to give it the middle finger and hoped Busty saw. A smile crossed my face as I imagined his reaction, but voices trickled from a room downstairs and my head snapped towards them, my smile collapsing as something crumpled and fragile replaced it. My breathing hitched; I stumble-walked faster, my palm flat on the wall to keep on my feet.

The stairs were intricate and perilous in a way they'd never been before, not even my wings affording me balance as I slowly made my way down them on unsteady legs. The louder my mates' voices grew, the tighter my throat became. I could hear Harvey, Kai, and Wyn, and when I reached the bottom of the stairs, I was surprised to realise they weren't arguing. They were bickering, but that was normal, and the TV echoed in the background, set on the news.

I paused outside the open door, my hand pressed to my chest as I listened.

"Get your foot off my fucking leg," Kai muttered.

"Get your leg off my foot," Harvey shot back, but strangely flat, empty of his usual smug amusement.

I peered around the doorway, finding Harvey and Kai on the sofa, Kai's expression gut-wrenching, his eyes swimming with misery. Not a single snake rippled the air around him. Harvey looked equally drawn, Wynvail now silent, sitting on the floor in front of the sofa.

Emlyn hunched in an armchair by the fire, his eyes unfocused on the flames. Wane stood at the window with Verena, their voices low and attention on the street outside, both their body language heavy with sadness and misery.

I swallowed, blinking fast. It was good to see Verena with them, to know even with me gone they'd remembered to look after her. She didn't have anyone else, and I knew how that felt. I'd have given my right arm back then for a family of smart-mouthed, smirking criminals with hearts of gold to take me in and give me a home.

A few days ago, I might have made a grand entrance, but I was too close to tears for that. I didn't even know why I was crying. I was back, I had my family. I should have been happy. But I wanted to curl into a ball and sob.

I padded into the room, my heart tight, emotions fragile.

"Em?" I breathed, swallowing the lump in my throat. "Can I have a hug?"

He glanced up, eyes still distant, but his arms were already opening. "Always, Hales."

The others were so distracted they didn't even look up as I climbed onto his lap and curled up, my head on his shoulder and tears finally spilling over. Tears of relief and pain blended, and the moment my scent hit Emlyn's senses, he jerked, his arms locking tighter around me as he gasped.

"Haley!" he blurted, loud enough that everyone else looked over.

Harvey fell off the sofa, immediately scrambling across the rug. Wynvail jumped to his feet and vaulted the coffee table, landing in front of me—and was knocked aside by Wane as he grabbed my face, frantic silver eyes searching me, pleading, disbelieving.

"I'm here," I said, thick with emotion.

Wane's thumbs brushed the tears from my cheeks, a hard breath punching out of his chest.

"I thought you were dead," Verena exclaimed, stumbling over to us and staring at me.

"I was," I replied, stroking Wane's back, squeezing Wynvail's shoulder, and brushing messy brown hair from Harvey's face. I needed more hands, goddammit.

A loud, shuddering sob snapped my panicked stare to Kai. He'd dropped his face into his hands and now his whole body shook, brutal, wrenching sobs shaking him.

"Come here, my night," I choked out, my heart breaking as I watched him shake and cry. "Kai."

A ragged, broken breath shook him as he uncurled on the sofa. Harvey moved, making room for Kai in front of me, and my sobbing mate dropped into it without a word. I turned on Em's lap, making sure his arms didn't unwrap from my waist, and the moment I touched Kai's face, his face crumpled and he bowed his head over me, clinging to my legs.

"How?" Harvey rasped, never once taking his eyes off me.

"I don't know," I replied, all my energy drained. "I should be dead."

"The pearl," Emlyn said, pulling me so my back was flush to his chest. "It has to be."

Wynvail shook his head, his jaw clenched as he fought back a tidal wave of feeling—I sensed it through the bond, sensed all of them. Even my mate bonds were intact, and that was a fucking miracle. Did I have Erebus to thank for that? "It should have been instant."

"What pearl?" I asked, a fresh wave of tears racing down my cheeks when I blinked.

"A resurrection pearl," Wynvail rasped, leaning into me when I stroked his hair. It wasn't quite as coiffed and neat as usual, and this time I actually hated seeing him rumpled, knowing grief was the reason. "It's a long story."

"It doesn't matter how you're back," Wane said, brushing tears off my cheeks. "All that matters is you're home."

My steady stream of tears became a dam burst of sobs when he pressed a kiss to my forehead, throwing me back into so many memories.

"Come here, kid," Emlyn murmured. "It's family group hug time."

I glanced up, giving Verena the best smile I could manage when I was a crying, snotty mess, and fluttered my hand at her, marvelling at how I could actually move and breathe and cry. "Get over here."

"Are you alright?" she asked, approaching tentatively, nothing like the fierce girl we first met, swearing and scornful through the stone wall between our cells.

"Strangely okay," I agreed, and decided to leave out the fact I was an emotional wreck, I was spiritually screaming, and mentally I was a tumbledown mess of stress, panic, questions, and traumatic memories. "Looks like we escaped unscathed."

Harvey made a throaty sound, his expression dark with intensity when I met his stare. Yeah, we'd all have a proper conversation later. When the truth wouldn't scare the shit out of Verena. I knew she was a tough kid but telling her everything that had happened would give her nightmares. Especially my death.

"Do I even want to know what happened after I—left," I said hoarsely, choking back another wail that clawed up my throat when Wynvail laced his fingers with mine, pressing a kiss to every joint and knuckle.

"Cronus is the king of the gods now," Wane said, hatred and panic fighting for dominance in his expression. "He has complete power."

I sighed. Of course he was, and of course he did. "But he thinks I'm dead, so he'll leave us alone, right?"

Kai flinched hard. I reached for him, stroking my thumb along his pale cheek, my chest collapsing at the devastation in his eyes. I wrapped my soul around his in the bond, holding tight, promising this was real, I was back, he hadn't lost me.

"We hope," Harvey muttered, still staring at me, not budging from where he knelt in front of the armchair.

"Good." I nodded decisively and pretended my breath didn't hitch and tears didn't drip off my chin. "That's done then. Game over. Happily ever after."

But we were crying and struggling to breathe, and it felt like a lie. We should have been happy, should have had the rest of our lives to live, but *it felt like a lie.*

CHAPTER 8

HARVEY

I didn't care that I hit rock bottom and sank to a whole new low; I followed Haley down the hallway from the living room to the bathroom, catching the door with my foot before it could close.

"Don't mind me," I said when she looked up, her pants and underwear halfway down her legs. "I'll just wait here."

She blinked.

"It's not the first time I've seen you pee, Sugarplum," I reminded her. It wasn't the first time I'd been clingy either, but this was on another level. "I couldn't breathe when you left my sight," I confessed, shutting the door and sitting my ass on the edge of the bath. "I'm sorry."

"Oh, Harvey," she sighed, shimmying her pants back up and leaning over to hug me. She squeezed tight enough that a knot unwound from my chest. I hugged her back too hard, too frantic. "What can I do? What do you need?"

"Just don't leave me," I answered quietly, my Adam's apple bobbing as I tried to swallow the lump in my throat.

I'd been on the verge of crying since I saw her sitting on Emlyn's lap, whole and healthy and alive, and now emotion scalded my face, a storm that could drown me. I couldn't choke it back, even though crying would only cause Haley more pain

I lost her. I fucking *lost* her. She was cold and still and dead, and my whole world just … stopped. Nothing moved, nothing breathed. Colour and joy and life just … stopped.

Every stereotypical, cliché thing anyone had ever said about grief was true, and even now, with her arms around me, I wanted to scream at the top of my lungs. It would be a long time before I accepted that she was here and breathing.

Even though I could touch her, feel her warmth, her breath stirring my hair, her scent in my lungs—bright and floral, not stagnant and dull—I couldn't forget how it felt to touch her hand and feel cold, slack skin, couldn't forget the emptiness in her eyes before they were closed or the way the bond just … stilled inside me. I didn't know why I didn't go feral this time. Feral would have been better than grieving.

"Harvey," she murmured, fingertips tracing my brow, brushing messy brown hair off my forehead. "It's okay now. I promise."

I focused my eyes on her, feeling sick. "Okay? I lost you," I managed to force past my swollen throat. *"I lost you,* Haley, you died, you were cold, you—"

A strangled cry stole the rest of my words, and she hugged me tighter, my head on her chest, her lips leaving kisses in my hair. My eyes burned and overflowed, and I clung to my mate, holding her so tightly that not even death could steal her from me.

"We're done," I choked out after long minutes, her arms never loosening around me, her kisses never stopping. "No more fights, no more titans, no more save the world bullshit. We're *done*."

"I know," she soothed, stroking my back with rough pressure, a weight falling off my shoulders at the touch. My wings drooped. "I know, Buttercup. It was never about saving the world; it was always about saving our family. But we're all safe, and we're staying the fuck out of anything else Cronus does."

The knot in my chest loosened at her easy agreement, and I tried to lighten my grip on her a fraction, so I didn't leave bruises on her newly healed body. Actually ... *was* she healed? I skimmed my hands down her sides, tilting my head up to kiss her jaw.

"Sorry in advance," I said against her skin, her scent wrapping around my tastebuds until she consumed me and something caved inside my chest.

"For what?" she murmured, and then hissed a vicious, creative curse that made me smile when I poured magic into her, coursing it through her ribs and down to the place where she'd stabbed herself. The wound was so deep and expansive that I faltered.

"Fuck, Haley," I whispered, tears flooding my face, hot and stinging.

"I couldn't let him win," she admitted quietly. "He was going to kill me anyway, but this way he couldn't consume me and grow even more powerful. I had a split second choice before he killed me, and I chose—"

"Spite," I finished, my voice raw. "You chose to spite him."

Haley froze, and I used the moment to pour my healing magic down her legs to the weakness at her ankle and search out more aches and pains, freeing her of even a single moment's discomfort.

"Are you mad at me?" she whispered.

I drew back, giving her a sharp look. "Are you crazy? If I

knew death was seconds away, I'd have chosen to spite the fucker, too." I tried to smile, and knew I failed miserably when she caught my hand and pulled it away from her stomach, kissing my knuckles.

"I love you," she said, her voice smaller, fragile.

The need to protect her surged, filling my chest to bursting, and a low vibrating growl formed in my chest. I guess I was a little feral after all. I bit back the growl and gentled my hold on her, tucking a strand of dirty pink hair behind her ear.

"I love you too, more than anyone or anything else in any world. You're the whole goddamn universe to me, Halwen Vakhara. If I lose you again, I won't survive it."

She nodded, a silent, tearful promise in her eyes to never leave me. "No more battles," she promised. "We're done. Only domestic bliss and a nice, harmless life from here on out."

"That better be a fucking promise," I muttered, my hand flat against her back, holding her close to me.

When she held out her hand, her little finger extended, a real smile softened my face. "It's a promise," she agreed when I linked our pinkies.

I sighed, exhaling my terror even if the grief wouldn't leave me for a long, long time. I slid my hand up and into her hair, bringing her lips to mine for a slow, thorough kiss.

When she groaned and melted into me, I finally accepted this wasn't an elaborate hallucination. She was alive. She was real.

When her taste overwhelmed my senses with sweetness, I gathered her close, her legs straddling me on the edge of the bath and my abs getting a serious workout from keeping us both from tumbling into the tub.

Her tongue claimed my mouth, her fingers grasping at my body and sinking into my hair in the same desperate movement. I cast off the worst of my pain. I had my mate back, and she wasn't going anywhere.

She shifted on my lap, a needy sound falling off her tongue onto mine, but she drew back to look at me. I couldn't read the look in her eyes, couldn't take my eyes off the flush of need on her face.

When she breathed, "You don't want me...?" my heart cracked in fucking two.

"What?" I tightened my hands on her, my stomach sinking at the fragility in her voice.

Oh. Oh, shit.

"Always, Haley. I *always* want you. I just—" I expelled a hard breath, kissing her softly. "My heart's too wrecked right now, and I can barely function, let alone get hard."

She swallowed and nodded, and it damn near killed me.

"I'm sure if you gave me a little strip tease, it might change things," I added cheekily, praying for a smile.

She rolled her eyes and shoved my shoulder, which was even better, even if I had to clench my stomach muscles to keep us on the edge of the bath and not splayed inside it.

"No? Not even in one of those scraps of lace I've seen in the drawer in your room? Wynvail might be an asshole, but he does have great taste in lingerie."

"They're pointless," she scoffed. "You can see my nipples through them."

"That's why I like them," I replied dryly, kissing the edge of her smile.

I jumped when a fist hammered on the door, and all my hard work at staying upright fell apart.

"Fuck," I shouted when gravity won the battle and dragged me into the tub, Haley splayed out on top of me. My head clattered it hard enough to make birds fly around my skull, but my mate was unhurt.

"Thanks, dickhead!" I yelled at the door.

Kai responded by ripping the door off its hinges, because of course he did. He flew into the bathroom in a fit of panic, his red eyes wide and searching.

"The door was unlocked," I drawled. "You didn't have to break it."

"Haley?" he demanded, sharp and fast. He threw himself at the bath, frantically pushing her hair aside so he could see her face.

"What?" she muttered, eyes slitted in irritation but that smile still on her face.

Kai exhaled hard, his glowing red eyes slamming shut. "You're okay."

"I'm laid in the bath," she drawled, "but otherwise fine. Help me out?"

Kai grasped her hand and pulled her out of the bath; I grunted when her knee met my kidney, giving Kai a narrow-eyed look. He didn't notice, his attention fixed on our mate, settling her safely on the floor in front of him, hands wandering over every part of her, reassuring himself she was still here, still unhurt, still alive.

I sighed roughly, sympathy clenching my chest as I pulled myself up.[1]

"I'll be in the living room," I told my mate, tugging on a strand of her hair. I tried to catch Kai's gaze to ask if he was alright, but his eyes were screwed shut, pain and relief cut deep into his sharp features.

"Take a shower, Sugarplum. I'll get some clothes for you."

"I still need to pee," she complained, but her hands stroked Kai's back and she didn't pull away.

It shredded my soul to walk away, but unfortunately for me I was a selfless bastard when it came to family. Kai needed time with her, too. Probably more than I did; he walked the scythe's edge of sanity at the best of times.

His reaction to losing Haley unsettled me. I'd never seen

him go so silent and empty before. Breaking shit, screaming, acting out with magic? Always. But silence, staring, and isolation? I didn't like it. But they'd take care of each other. Even though it cut me up, I put one foot in front of the other and left the bathroom.

"How is she?" Wane demanded the second I slumped into the living room.

"Alive," I replied, going over to my brother and wishing I knew how to ask for a hug.

I must have looked pretty pathetic because he drew me close and squeezed me in a hug without me speaking a single word.

"Right now, that's all we can ask for," I finished.

CHAPTER 9

KAI

"Shh," Haley murmured, holding me close as my body collapsed, a wrecking ball destroying my chest until all I felt was pain, crashing through my stomach until I felt sick. "It's okay, I'm okay."

The bathroom blurred, the violently rainbow shower curtain smearing across my sight until it taunted me, so fucking colourful when my whole world was black.

"Kai—"

I lurched aside, bowing over the sink a moment before vomit burned my throat and my stomach cramped, expelling bile. I hadn't eaten anything, so it was acid that scalded my throat and splattered across the porcelain.

Another wave of nausea ravaged my stomach when Haley stroked my back, murmuring words of reassurance when I started to shake, the vibrations deep and out of control. When her soul brushed mine, the bond healthy and strong between us, my knees buckled. I gripped the edge of the sink hard, holding myself up through sheer force.

"Don't lock it up," she breathed, pushing sweaty red hair out of my face when I continued to shake even after I stopped throwing up. "Let your emotions out, Kai. I can feel them tearing you apart."

I bowed over the porcelain and dry heaved, nauseated and cold. Haley was behind me, touching me, but a thousand miles away.

"Maybe I deserve to be torn apart," I said so quietly I didn't expect her to hear me.

"Come on," she said, softness swapped for decisiveness as she pulled me from the sink and towards the mammoth shower in the corner. What bathroom needed a giant shower and a bath big enough for three? This whole house was overkill.[1] "Get in," she ordered, bustling me into the cubicle fully dressed and reaching for the fancy touch-screen pad on the wall.

"Haley," I sighed in complaint, jumping when water drummed down on me, freezing cold before it warmed, scorching my skin and bones.

"Stay here. And face the wall. Why does no one think I'm serious when I say I need a fucking piss?"

That was one of those things I knew I should have laughed at, but I just turned to the wall and rested my forehead against it, letting the water drown my clothes until my body felt as heavy as my heart.

I barely processed time passing, my head tipped down and numbness starting to spread through my body now the sickness had abated. Maybe Haley was right and my emotions were tearing me apart, but I couldn't feel a single one of them. I couldn't feel the barbed edges of my grief at losing her, or the wobbly relief at having her back, not a single spark of happiness or irritation or—anything.

I jumped when arms slid around me from behind. Haley's voice was muffled and deep, but her words were alien when she spoke to me. I couldn't make out a single word, and my tongue was too thick and heavy to ask her what she'd said. Did it matter anyway? She died. My mate died. I held her limp body, kissed her cold forehead, and screamed until my voice gave out and silence filled every part of me. How long would she stay this time? A month? A week? A day? Death would come for her. I was never allowed to keep anything good and pure.

Firm hands pulled at me, and I let her manoeuvre me in the shower, pushing me until I sat beneath the water's spray. I couldn't even tell if it was hot or cold, it just soaked me to the bone, slicked my hair to my cheeks and forehead, and dripped from my lips like poison kisses.

Haley spoke again, her voice deep and garbled. I couldn't stand it, couldn't stand the sight of her when I knew I'd lose her again, couldn't bear her scent in my lungs and the feel of her hands imprinted on my body. It hurt—every scent, every hug, every word. They hurt like hell, and I was too weak to endure it.

Haley moved my legs until she could kneel between them, her hands catching my numb face and lifting it. *Look at me.* I saw her lips move, knew the words even if I couldn't hear anything but a blur of noise.

I swallowed, my eyes fixed on her chin where an old scar nicked her skin, so small but as familiar as any scar on my own body.

She was here and real and I couldn't accept it. The second I did, she'd be ripped away from me again.

I gasped when she pulled me close, the heat and feel of her making the entire foundation of my being tremble like it did when she held me from behind. Gentle fingers carded through my wet hair, pressing my face against her shoulder, my nose so close to her neck where her scent was inescapable.

My stomach churned, my eyes burning. We were both covered in water; she wouldn't notice if I cried, would she? I let the tears fall, scalding my eyeballs before they dropped onto her skin, washed away with the rest of the water.

Murmurs blurred in my ears as she held me close, not caring that we were both dressed and soaked through. She held the back of my neck in a firm enough grip that I felt it even through my numbness, and more tears fell.

I was going to be sick again; I could feel it in the twist of my stomach and the sharp ache in my chest, burrowed deep into my soul. I wanted to scream again, wanted to sob, but I swallowed the sounds and—

I knew those words. My breath caught as the rough blur of noise resolved into words in my native language, one line repeated over and over, *promised* over and over.

A small sound choked in my throat and I sniffled, tears flowing faster.

I will always be your shadow and light; you will always be my rose and life.

I didn't realise she knew them by heart. My face collapsed; I buried it in her shoulder and cut off every pained sound that tried to claw its way free.

"Let it out, my night," she murmured, her thumb stroking circles on the back of my neck, making my breath catch. Like the hitch gave it a chokehold, a sob tore free, followed by another, and then five, until I didn't stand a chance of holding them back. "I'm here, I'm here, let it all out."

A sharp, keening cry shook my chest when she spoke our promise again, her pronunciation clumsy and soft, making my stomach cave in. I clung to her with shaky, still numb hands and wished I could feel her, wished I felt her fingers as more than a faint brush in my hair. Her scent filled my lungs with every sobbing breath, taunting me with what I'd lost.

I couldn't accept it. That she was back, that she was right in front of me. Relief crushed me when I first saw her, sitting on Em's lap like it was a normal day, but I didn't feel that relief anymore. I couldn't feel anything but emptiness and pain and—fear.

"I'm not going anywhere," she promised like she knew exactly what I was feeling. "Do you hear me, Kai? I'm here, and I'm staying. No more fighting titans, no more god shit. I won't even go to Hell to talk to my friends, because they're right in the thick of all that bullshit, and I'll just be drawn back in."

Something squirmed in my soul—her emotion.

"What?" I asked, hoarse and tight. "What is it?"

"Lucifer is dead. Cronus ate him. I meant what I said, I'll stay away, but ... Lili's gotta be messed up right now."

"Everyone's messed up," I rasped, her words clearer to me now, their meaning easy instead of sluggish.

She exhaled a rough sigh, pulling back from me and gazing at the wreckage of my face. "Kai..."

"It won't work," I told her, too afraid to meet her eyes. "This. Holding me, talking to me. It won't work. I died right there with you, Haley."

"But I came back," she said in a small voice. "Please look at me."

I shook my head, the numbness wearing off and exposing the tangle of pain and misery and sickness underneath. "No."

"What are you scared of, Kai? I'm right here. I swear it's not a trick or a lie. I'm really here."

"For how long?" I tried to shift her away, to rise to my feet, but she wouldn't let me. If I'd called up my magic, I could have moved her with a single snake, but that part of me, like my heart, was hollowed out.

"What?" she whispered.

"How long until the next death? How long until you don't come back? How long until—until we have to bury you and throw dirt on your coffin and walk away forever?" My voice broke. Shit.

She shook her head, her throat bobbing. "Not gonna happen. We're done with anything and everything that could ever hurt us. We're *done*, Kai. Not even a damn bar fight."

When I just stared at the place her thighs brushed mine, she asked, "Do you think I *want* to die again? Don't you think I was terrified, Kai? You know I still have nightmares of the first time we were killed, and this time was—worse." She sucked in a sharp breath, her chest jumping. "The first time, I was alive one moment and the next, there was nothing. No blackness, no white light. Nothing."

I knew. I'd experienced the same thing. My hands flexed, palms tingling; I rested them on her waist, sweeping my thumbs over the curve of her hip, and a new wave of tears squeezed out of my stinging eyes at the feel of her under my hands—hot and soft and familiar.

But if I accepted this was real, I opened myself up to losing her again. And I would; it was all I'd ever done. Love her and lose her.

"This time," she said, swallowing, "it wasn't instant. I felt my life being stolen, and it took a whole fucking eternity of pain until everything finally went dark. I heard—I heard Em screaming. I felt your pain—yours and Harvey's. I'm sorry, Kai. I know you're angry, and I'm so sorry."

"I'm not angry," I said. "I don't feel anything."

"Kai," she said, pained, and pulled me into a tight hug. Now the numb had worn off, I felt every indentation of her fingertips on my shoulders, felt the rapid beat of her heart against my chest and the quick, panicked rush of her breathing. Why was she panicked?

I dared a quick glance at her face and sucked in a sharp breath at the ocean of misery in her eyes. Fuck. I pulled in a slow breath and shoved my way through the tangled mess in my chest, reaching for her soul. I jumped in surprise, snapping my arms around her and dragging her flush against me. She wasn't just panicked; she was absolutely petrified, terror bleeding through her soul like shards of ice and venom, making every part of her it touched wilt and cry.

"I'm not angry," I repeated, some emotion seeping into my voice even as I flinched from it. If I let myself love her, unreserved, it would kill me when I lost her.

But if I held back, it would kill her now, while she lived.

"Not with you, my rose," I added, deciding honestly was the best policy. "With the world? With the monster who forced your hand? With myself for not glueing to your side? Yes. You? *No.*"

I wasn't angry. I was hurt and confused and insecure, but her soul was all around me and I knew if I spoke those feelings, she couldn't handle it. She was barely holding herself together, probably pushed close to a breakdown by our grief piling on top of her own.

"It's not your fault," she argued. "Nothing you could have done would stop it. You'd have died with me and—and you might not have come back."

I wanted to push the subject, but a tremor went through her soul at the thought of me dying and I choked down the words, holding her tighter.

"Talk to me," she pleaded after minutes of silence, only the water drumming around us. "Please, Kai."

I tipped my head back so water cascaded down my face, the pressure hard enough that it felt punishing. "I can't."

"It's going to torture you," she breathed.

"My mate died. I'm already tortured."

She nodded, blinking fast. "I came back. I—I remembered

you, and I came back. In the darkness, I could have just ...
slipped away and never come home, but I saw my mates. I saw
you, following me from the safe house that night, giving me
my daggers, kissing me until nothing else mattered."

Her voice choked off. My eyes burned, my teeth clenched
as emotion ravaged every one of my weaknesses, clawing into
my soul.

"I'll lose you again," I bit out. "I always do. You're ripped
away from me every fucking time, and I—"

My voice twisted, a strangled, broken thing, and I ducked
my head as I lost control.

Haley brushed wet crimson hair away from my ear and
cradled my head to her chest. "Listen," she urged. *"Listen,* Kai.
I'm here, and I'm not going anywhere. You can come watch
me pee with Harvey if you want, I don't care. Just tell me what
you need, because I'm not going fucking anywhere."

I gripped her tight, my breathing fast and wrecked, but the
rapid thud of her heart met my ears, drowned out every other
side, and I had to clench my jaw to stop another destructive
wave of tears.

"Haley," I rasped, the shower shuddering as my magic
quaked through me. I jumped when she tugged a lock of my
hair, hard enough that sensation flashed across my scalp.

"Stop holding back. If you need to cry, cry."

Her voice was every bit as stern as her grip on my hair. "I
don't want to cry."

"Tough shit. Do it."

I laughed, a sob escaping on the tail of the sound. "My
cruel rose."

I clenched my jaw tighter, the echoing thud of her heart in
my ears, every *thud-thud* breaking down my walls until the
trembling, terrified thing they hid threatened to escape. My
hands flexed, holding her too tightly, and I unclenched them

instantly, panic shooting through me like a falling star. What if I hurt her? What if I lost her again because I was too careless?

Fuck. She was really here, really back, and all I was doing was hurting her. She wasn't safe with me—

"What's going through your head, Kai?" she asked, her voice harder. "I can feel your panic escalating. Talk to me. And this time it's non-negotiable; we're not leaving this shower until you tell me what you're thinking."

I swallowed, the thump of her heartbeat driving into me like a punch to the gut every time. She was alive, and real, and I was fucking this up. The thought of telling her about the mess in my head made me want to throw up, but if talking was what she wanted, I could suck it up and talk.

"This doesn't feel real," I said quietly, only brave enough to confess it because my face was hidden in her chest. "I know it is, I can feel you through the bond, and I—I'm starting to accept that you're here, you're back with me. But it doesn't feel real. I'm—I'm *grieving* you, Haley, and you're right here but I'm still grieving you."

Her breath hitched. She held me fiercer. "I hate that you're hurting."

"I'm hurting because I love you," I said, swallowing, "and I'll never regret that. But losing you has me fucked up and I—I don't think I can be the Kai you love right now."

Fingers gripped my hair so hard I hissed; she pulled my head off her chest so I could witness the glorious scowl on her face. Fuck, I loved her. I missed her. I needed her.

"The fact that you think I only love one part of you makes me want to force feed you untoasted marshmallows, Malakai Virex."

I made a face, already feeling the gross non-melty texture on my tongue. "Anything but that, my rose."

"I love every fucking part of you," she went on as if I never spoke, her voice rough and coarse with a sexy little growl in it. "There's not a single part of you I don't love, so I don't care if you need space to process your grief, or if you need me closer than ever, or if you need to plan an emotional support bank robbery. Just—tell me what you need."

"I thought we were banned from crime and fights," I pointed out dryly.

"I'll break the rules for you," she replied quickly, her face softening, her stormy eyes big and bright with pain—my pain. "I'll break every rule for you."

My breath caught. I lifted a hand, skimming my knuckles along her jaw and trying so fucking hard not to fight the burning in my eyes. I was terrified to let the emotion out. It would run through me like a hurricane and leave only wreckage but—Haley needed me to be open. So I unclenched my jaw, let out a ragged exhale, and allowed a scalding tear free on my next blink.

"If I—" I began but didn't know how to put my fear into words. Haley's fingers ran through my hair, gentle now. "If I accept that you're back, if I let all this shit festering in my chest out—there's no going back, there's nothing to protect me, I'll be weak and exposed and—I'm fucking scared, Haley. I'm scared to lose you and scared to die because I won't survive losing you a third time, and I'm scared what losing us both will do to our family and I'm just—I—"

A tear burned a hot line down my cheek, and I screwed my eyes shut when Haley kissed it away, her lips lingering on my skin.

"If I don't talk about this, I don't have to face it. I don't have to admit that we're damned, and there's no doubt something else will come to kill us. If I lock everything inside, I can pretend we'll be fine, I'll never lose you and—"

I throttled the words in my throat.

"I can't help you," she finished, kissing my other cheek. "If you don't talk about it. The pain won't go away, but you'd have to face it alone. I'm *your mate*, Kai. This is the whole point of my existence; to help you shoulder your burdens and kick the shit out of your problems and make you happy when the whole world falls apart. I'm your mate, Kai."

I tipped my head back against the shower wall, releasing a hard breath. She was my mate—and I was hers. It was my job to protect her and make her happy, too.

I feathered my thumb across her cheek and felt it like a kick to the stomach when her eyes welled. "So how do we kick the shit out of my problems when we're not allowed to kill the bastard who created them?"

"We do the opposite. We stay very fucking far from him. We never see him again."

"I want him to suffer," I confessed, forcing myself to speak my thoughts. "I want to torture him, over and over, until he screams and cries and feels even one iota of the torment I've felt since I lost you. No, fuck that—since Aphrodite kidnapped you on his obvious command. He owes too much for me to let it lie."

Haley dropped her gaze. "You sound like I did when I got us killed, when I pushed for us to kill Locke before he could hurt us. We can't do that again."

I sighed, the wind knocked swiftly from my sails.

"No," I agreed. "We can't."

Everything started that day. Locke killed us, separating us from Haley, from Wane, creating Wynvail to trick us into freeing the titan bastard from his prison, leading to everything that happened in Olympus. Every nightmare that had happened could be traced back to the trap Locke sprang around us in the Damned Realm.

Another rough breath punched out of my lungs. I felt the humanity returning to me, the numbness wearing off completely until I just felt weak. Hollow and broken and *weak*.

"So, no revenge," I said, settling my arms around my mate again and allowing myself to appreciate that she was warm and solid under my hands. I'd never been a coward, so why was I so scared to fully embrace her? Why was I holding back? It wouldn't protect me. It wouldn't make it hurt any less if she was ripped away from me. "What do we do instead?"

Her shoulders slumped, and I realised my rose had walls of her own up when all her fierce protectiveness gave way to something weary and exhausted and sad. Her pain pressed on my soul, compounding my own, but she had five souls full of grief and agony in her chest.

"Make pancakes? Beef stew? Spaghetti?" she suggested, so tired it was hard to hear.

I pulled her against my chest and squeezed tight, curving my hand around the back of her head and dropping a long kiss in her hair. "You unknowingly entered into a bargain by making me talk about my grief," I told her, dropping my next kiss on the beautiful arch of her black wing.

"I did?"

"Mm," I agreed. "You're now bound by the terms and conditions of our bargain to let out your own emotions. I know you're holding back because you're worried about all of us, but you're carrying our grief on top of your own suffering. There's no way death magically wiped away all your stress of being imprisoned and then fighting for your life. You're still in survival mode, no matter how well you're hiding it, and I'm willing to bet your emotions are even more fucked up by killing yourself and then coming back. Correct me if you're wrong."

She sniffled, and my heart lurched when hot tears met my shoulder, scalding compared to the now-balmy warmth of the shower.

"I'm tired of fighting, Kai. I'm tired of feeling scared and exhausted and waiting for the next god or monster to show up and attack us. I've had enough."

I stroked down her wings with slow, gentle touches, choking back my own agony at her words. They made me murderous, made me want to hunt down everyone who'd ever harmed her, cut them apart, and rip all their organs out through the gaping slashes.

"Definitely beef stew," I said when I'd controlled my rage. "You need comfort food. So stew, dumplings, and let's have spaghetti, too. Fuck it. We can have pancakes, cake, and ice cream for dessert."

"How big do you think my stomach is?" she laughed, the sound choked.

I laid another kiss on her crown, part of me settling enough for me to open the bond more, to show her more of me. She sniffled again, a hitched breath that told me she was crying hard.

"We'll be okay," I promised, and wondered how the fuck I'd got here from the empty denial I'd been in minutes ago. "It doesn't feel like it, but we'll be okay, my rose."

I inhaled my first full breath in days, the weight on my chest starting to ease.

"I love you so much it should be physically impossible," I said, tightening my arms around her. "You're half of my soul, my whole goddamn world, and I swear, no one will ever hurt you again. Including you. Understood?"

"Understood," she choked out, and my stomach dropped. Fuck, I'd been too hard on her, I'd—

She drew back, and she was smiling. Tears tracked down her cheeks, but she was smiling, her eyes creased and shining. "I love you, Malakai. I don't know what I'd do without you."

"You never have to find out."

Haley sighed, tension relaxing from her, her smile still in

place. At least until a fist hammered on the bathroom door. It was either Wane or Em; they were the only ones with enough manners to knock instead of just bursting in.

"Something's happening," Wane called through the door. "It's on the TV. We need to come up with an evacuation plan."

Evacuation? For fuck's sake! Would we ever get a fucking break?

PART II
PART 2 - SHADE

CHAPTER 10

HALWEN

I wasn't entirely serious about the domestic bliss thing, so it was trippy as fuck to watch Emlyn and Wynvail peacefully coexist in the kitchen, a shopping bag of newly delivered ingredients open on the white marble island as Em mixed up a batch of pancakes and Wyn browned meat in a pan for stew. None of us were speaking about the herd of elephants in the room. Plural.

- I'd died—and come back.
- Wynvail had died—and come back.
- Verena stared into space, far too quiet.
- We were all mid-mental-breakdown.
- Our king had been eaten, and Hell was falling apart.
- And our enemy had more power than ever.

Harvey rummaged through the shopping bag, his hip pressed to mine, the physical contact the only thing grounding him. He came up with a carrot that had a bulbous root that looked suspiciously like a dick and balls.

I smirked. "Must be an organic carrot."

"An organdick carrot," he joked, earning a groan from the entire room.

"That's fucking awful," Kai muttered, slouched against the fridge across the room, his eyes branded on me and refusing to budge.

"I'd like to hear you do much better," Harvey quipped, throwing the carrot at him. Kai ducked; it smacked into the fridge.

Wynvail snapped his hand out and caught it before it met the floor, turning to give both of them a foreboding look. "If you fuck up *any* of my food, I'll poison the both of you."

"As if," Verena scoffed, standing in the doorway watching the tableau with her arms crossed over her chest and a vacant look in her eyes. She was paying attention though; she was listening. I really hoped that was a good sign. I didn't know how to take care of an obviously traumatised teenager when I was equally traumatised. "If you poison them, Haley will be pissed, and you'd never risk that."

Wynvail turned to her, an eyebrow raised. "Interesting assessment."

"Accurate assessment," she threw back, but there was something too forced about the attitude in her voice.

Wynvail scoffed, washing and cutting up the carrot. "I can make decisions without taking my mate into account for every one."

"Can you?" Emlyn drawled, making a smile tug at my mouth. "Give me that," he huffed at Harvey when he pulled a knobbly potato from the bag and snorted. In his defence, it did look like an ass, complete with a crack and two butt cheeks.

Em cuffed Harvey across the head and passed Wynvail the

potato, and it was such a normal action that another knot unwound from my chest. But—where was Wane?

I searched for him in the mess of my soul and found his location—close, maybe a few rooms away—but not a hint of emotion. Wane had been open and raw for days, his walls shattered by a hundred years of Cronus's torture. The fact that he'd now walled himself off from me was a bad sign.

"Back in a minute," I told everyone in the kitchen and tugged one of Verena's red pigtails when I squeezed past her out the door.

"Why does everyone keep doing that?" she spat, throwing a scowl at me.

"Because you're cute."

I glanced up when Kai and Harvey moved to follow me, and whatever anxiety had loosened in my chest tightened all over again. "I won't be long," I promised them. "I'm just going to find Wane."

Harvey's bronze throat bobbed, his nostrils flaring as he fought his panic, but he nodded.

Kai just stared at me and stopped halfway across the kitchen, tension in every line of his body. His eyes glowed, dark, dark red—far deeper than usual.

"Kai," I breathed, sending him a gentle brush through the bond. "Please."

"One minute," he said, his voice low and foreboding.

"Ten," I countered, brushing against that iron wall Wane had thrown up around his emotions.

"One," Kai growled, never looking away from me.

I flicked my tongue over my dry bottom lip, every part of my chest filling with pain—mine, theirs, then my own sympathy for their grief. It was a bloody mess of thorns and barbs and every time I moved, I opened more wounds.

"Five," Emlyn input, worried blue eyes flicking between us. "Come help me with this spaghetti, Kai. Harvey, get the berries out of the bag since you're so interested in its contents. You can make the compote for the pancakes."

I shot Em a grateful glance, letting my love bleed through my eyes. He returned it with his softest, most affectional look, and I had to clench my jaw to stop my bottom lip wobbling. I'd been a second away from bursting into tears since I woke up three hours ago, and the emotion showed no signs of fading.

"How can I help?" I heard Verena ask as I hurried down the hallway, following my tether to Wane. "I can cook."

That was the best bit of news I'd heard all day. We had another cook—that made three, thanks to Wynvail knowing how to grill meat and vegetables without burning them to a crisp. The rest of us were abysmal.

No one was mentioning what we'd seen on the TV, or the argument we'd had after. We'd decided to stay and hope the protections on the safe house held, rather than fleeing somewhere new with no guarantee of safety, but no one was particularly happy.

Meteorologists had noticed a strange weather phenomena sweeping across Europe, originating in Greece. The night had been uncommonly long for the past two nights, the days unusually short, and instead of a sunset, night had fallen instantly like a black cover cast over a birdcage. And every day got shorter, like the night was swallowing it. That would have been unsettling enough without the fact the leaders of each country the dark swept over was forced to kneel, like their legs had given out, at the exact moment the shadow passed over it. The president of France, chancellor of Germany, royal family of Spain, first minister of Scotland, and prime minister of England were all sent to their knees, one after the other, like dominoes.

Like my mates described happening on Olympus when

Cronus made himself ultimate king of the gods. King of the world, apparently.

Hence, we were staying right here, where it was warded and safe.

I found Wane in the living room by the window, an empty tumbler in his hand, the fancy crystal kind because Wynvail was bougie as fuck.

"Wane?" I asked quietly, not wanting to spook him.

He glanced over his shoulder, a furrow between his dark brows. "I thought you were in the kitchen with the others."

"I was." I crossed the room slowly, trying to gauge his mood. "I missed you."

He set the empty glass on the windowsill and lifted his arm in silent invitation. I approached slowly, scanning his face and hating the tiredness lining it even as relief made my shoulders slump at the sight of him unharmed and free. The scars all over his body were inescapable reminders of what he'd been through, but they were evidence of his strength and love. I didn't baulk from the sight of them, but I did hesitate to touch him.

"Are you sure?" I asked.

In response he reached out and hooked his hand around my waist, pulling me into him with a dominance that reminded me of how he fucked me in the bathroom. He shattered my whole world apart that night in the best of ways.

"I'm sure, itzaia," he promised, kissing my cheek and surrounding my senses with the strong scent of whiskey. That definitely wasn't his first drink.

"Honest answer," I murmured, looking into his quicksilver eyes. "Are you drunk?"

"Not nearly enough," he replied, his hand flexing on my waist, pulling me closer. A deep sigh left him, and he rested his chin on top of my head.

"Let me in, zivai," I murmured, sending a brush down our bond.

"Your soul is full of pain, Haley," he replied. "I won't add to it."

"I can handle it," I argued. "I can't handle you closing off the bond."

"I just need a little time to process everything," he promised, drawing back a little and tipping my head back so our gazes met. "I'm not shutting you out, Haley, I'm putting you first. As I should, as your mate." He dropped a kiss on my cheek. "Don't worry about me; compared to the others, I'm fine."

I gave him a stern look. "Don't bullshit me, Van Khama."

"Don't underestimate me, Vakhara," he fired back, dropping a lingering kiss on my lips. "I can handle this. I've been scared for a century; this is nothing."

Except it was his abuser being unleashed on the world, with ultimate power and endless reach. Cronus had tortured Wane while *inside his prison.* If he was that bad trapped, how bad would it be with him free?

"It's not nothing," I argued softly. "And it's okay to be scared, Wane. You'd be mad if you weren't. I'm scared, too."

I stroked up his sides, careful to avoid the places his wings had been severed from him. Images flashed through my head —Wane kneeling before Cronus's throne, the bastard hacking off his wings, Cronus sitting smugly on his throne while my mate's wings hung from the wall above him.

I sucked in a breath, shaking my head to dislodge the images. Erebus was right; I shouldn't have seen that.

"Haley?" Wane's hands tightened on my body; he stared intensely, scanning my face. "What is it?"

My throat bobbed. I glanced away. I'd told them that when my soul separated from my body, instead of floating off to an afterlife, Erebus intercepted it and kept me safe until I was ready to come back. I hadn't told them most of what we said or saw in the darkness.

"I'm sorry," I blurted, my stomach twisting. "I'm so sorry, Wane."

"Hey," he breathed, folding me back into his arms and wrapping a layer of shadows around us both. "You have nothing to apologise for."

My airway closed off, and I was glad he was holding me so I didn't have to look him in the eye. "I saw him—I saw him take—"

"Take what?" he asked gently, tendrils of his magic caressing me until I wanted to drop to my knees and beg his forgiveness.

"Your wings," I whispered, choked. "I'm so sorry, I shouldn't have seen—"

"How?" he asked, his voice deep and gruff.

I choked back a rush of tears, letting go of him and stepping back. My eyes burned harder when his shadows clung to me, refusing to let go.

"When I was in the darkness with Erebus, he kept showing me things that would make me come back, kept nagging me to remember, to fight when I wanted to just give up. He told me about Cronus and the beginning of the universe, then the creation of the Earth, the rise of the titans, the fall of the gods. Whenever he mentioned Cronus, I got so angry. Rage took over, until one time he mentioned what that monster did to you and—I'm so sorry."

Wane grabbed his empty glass from the windowsill and screwed off the cap of the whiskey bottle, pouring an amount I was pretty sure was three shots worth. He downed half of it in a second and didn't even cough.

"I never wanted you to know any of it," he said roughly, the glass shaking in his hand. "Not a single thing that happened to me."

I gritted my teeth, like a damn holding back a flood. "I know."

"But you saw—?" When I nodded, his eyes slammed shut, devastation crossing his face. "Which parts? Tell me."

"I saw ... I saw someone cut your wings from your back."

"Andryas Revairs," Wane spat, his face twisted. He looked like he wanted to spit the taste of the name from his mouth. "My jailor. Cronus's previous pet, and current slave."

My bottom lip shook even with my teeth clenched. Fuck.

"That was all you saw?" he asked, an intensity shining through his molten silver eyes when he looked at me. I met his eyes for a second and then glanced away, so guilty I was going to throw up. "Nothing else?"

"Just ... them being cut. And—Cronus hung them on the wall. That's all I saw."

He exhaled a breath, and panic made my entire body freeze in place. I saw someone hack his wings off his back, saw him scream and howl and cry—and he was relieved that was all I'd seen. What else? What else had been done to him?

Kai was right. We needed revenge. Cronus needed to suffer for an eternity.

My heart beat faster, terror and guilt overruled by pure, burning rage. Wane sucked in a breath when my curse marks began to glow. They were both broken, the first by Oren's tattoo and the second by my god-killers, but the magic was every bit as potent as before. It responded to my fury, glowing brighter, casting red across the drinks cabinet, the window, and over the sofas and chairs until everything was stained crimson.

"What else?" I asked, my voice low and resonant. "What else did he do, Wane? What are you scared I'll see?"

He shook his head and threw back the rest of the whiskey in his glass. "Nothing."

"Don't lie. Please."

He glanced at the ceiling, fighting an emotion I couldn't place. "I can't tell you. Haley, please."

Magic crashed back into my body, and I jolted at the raw plea in his voice. He was *begging* me. Fuck. All my rage fled, leaving oily guilt and fear coursing through me.

"It's okay." I shook my head. "Of course you can't, it's okay. I'm so sorry. It's just—the thought of what could have been done to you makes me want to burn the whole world down."

I took a slow breath when Wane stayed silent, composing myself, trying to be strong for both of us. All of us.

When he was triggered before, sparring had helped him recover, but I knew it was more about him being in control of his actions that had made the difference.

So I swallowed and said, "Stay here. I'll be back in a second," and rushed from the room, racing down the hall and up the stairs to the training room. It was full of weapons Wynvail had stocked, but also my own. I grabbed one I'd procured in Iarlon[1] and curled my fingers around the hilt—a spiral of smooth metal, topped with a long, wicked blade.

"Here," I panted, sprinting back into the living room and surprised Kai hadn't burst into the room yet. We had to be nearing five minutes and there was no way my psycho mate wasn't timing me to the second.

"A knife," Wane murmured when I flipped it in my hand and held out the hilt. His scarred fingers wrapped around it, my name stark against his skin, and I swallowed back a thousand different words.

"You know I'll kill anyone who's ever hurt you," I panted, seriously out of breath. I blamed it on dying.[2] "But if I can't be at your side and you feel unsafe, or you can't ask for help or speak about what's torturing you—I want you to keep this on you always. I'll find a sheath that fits you. It's a promise, Wane. You're safe, and I'll always protect you—but you can use the knife to stab your enemies in the throat yourself. You're a badass, too. Just in case you've forgotten."

He looked at the knife, silent for so long that my stomach got tangled up again and my eyes burned.

"This is yours," he said after a second that felt like eternity. "You had it in Iarlon."

"It's yours now." I dared to take a step forward; his shadows reached for me again, brushing my legs, creeping up to wrap around my thigh. "A reminder that you're not helpless, you're not a victim. And it kinda reminds me of that knife you had in Szivah, when you cut off that letch's balls."

He laughed abruptly, seeming surprised at the sound. "I'd forgotten that."

"I recall it fondly. It turns me on."

His expression warmed, his eyes rising to me. I yelped in surprise when his shadows wrenched me close, pressing me against his body as his arms came around me, knife angled away.

"I know it does. I remember how you rewarded me afterward."

I groaned, dropping my head onto his shoulder as heat flashed through me. He'd sat at the bottom of the bed, as close as he could get, his hand wrapped around his hard cock as he stared at the place my fingers plunged into my pussy, so wet I'd soaked the sheets under me. When he came it had splashed my skin, as close to touch as we ever got. It was hot as fuck.

"I came like ... six times that night," I muttered. "I nearly passed out."

When I lifted my head, there was a very self-satisfied look on Wane's face, and I swallowed, my body hotter still.

He kissed me suddenly, hot and fast, his hand moulding to my cheek while his arm locked around me, keeping me trapped for him to kiss thoroughly senseless. The brush of the knife's hilt at my back only heightened everything. He only dragged his lips away when I was gasping, every part of me scalded, quivering, throbbing.

"I'm not mad about what you saw. I don't like that you witnessed it, but you already knew it had happened. Tell me if you need to talk about what you saw, okay?"

I nodded, panting, slowly piecing my wits back together. "Are they—still in that place?"

"I don't know." He kissed my cheek and stepped back, reaching for his glass to refill it. I caught his hand and wrapped it around his other, both curled around the knife's hilt. He sighed, but his gaze was warm, understanding my silent plea.

We both jumped when Kai exploded into the room, his eyes finding me like a heat-seeking missile. "Your five minutes are up."

I suspected he'd given us longer, but I didn't point that out. "We're coming," I said, and linked my arm with Wane's, tugging him through the living room like the bossy bitch I was.

He dropped another kiss on the top of my head as we walked, and I knew I was forgiven.

CHAPTER 11

WYNVAIL

*I*t had to be here somewhere. I pushed another dusty wooden box aside on the high shelf and squinted, balancing precariously on a chair I stole from the dining room. I already had a smear of dust on the right leg of my grey sweatpants, and I was pissed about it.

"Come on, you elusive bastard," I muttered, propping the lid on the next box and shoving it away when it didn't contain the glass bottle I was looking for.

I knew it was in this room; I distinctly remembered putting it safely in a box when I purchased it. But it had been decades since, and the room was a mess of clutter.

This whole room was my secret weapon, my true armoury, but anyone would take one look at it and see a hoarder's paradise. Shelves overflowed magical objects, stretching all the way from floor to ceiling; cabinets full of delicate porcelain, ancient iron, and rarer materials strained at the glass doors; potion bottles fought for space on a worktable against the back wall; and the entire left wall was full of jars full of plants and herbs that promised to empower their user with a thousand different traits and strengths. Some of them glowed, others appeared dull and ordinary; others still swallowed all the light inside their bottles until the glass was as black as a void.

It was my favourite room, and no one had ever known about it. It really shouldn't have surprised me when the door creaked and Haley propped herself against the door frame, surveying the tall-ceilinged space. She was wearing someone's shirt; three sizes too big for her, it hit mid-thigh but left the rest of her curvy legs bare. She was barefoot with her long pink hair falling loose over her shoulders, all tanned, inked skin, the shirt a temptingly thin barrier. Fuck.

She let out a low whistle. "Starting an antiques business?"

"No," I muttered, grabbing the next box and propping the lid, "and the mere thought of selling any of this makes me want to kill someone."

"So it's your hoard," she mused. "Like a surly dragon."

"Like a made thing with a master who's invincible," I corrected, scanning the set of ancient spoons in the box before replacing the lid and reaching for the next one. "This is my life's work, although I've made a piss poor job of adding to it lately. The pin I stole from you was stolen from me before I could hide it here."

"That's ironic," she drawled.

"Come inside and shut the door," I instructed, spearing her with a commanding look. "No one else can know about this place, only us."

"And the others," she argued.

"Fine," I muttered, knowing this was a fight I wouldn't win. "But not the kid. If she gets into any of this, it could have disastrous consequences. End of the world shit. Or end of *her* shit."

"Understood," she murmured, pushing the door shut behind her and slowly walking into the room, eyes scanning, searching, devouring the space.

"And don't you touch anything either, Halwen. Your hand could melt off if you touch the wrong thing."

She winced. "Eek."

I couldn't believe she'd just said the word *eek*. She didn't even make the sound; she spoke it like a word. I battled to keep the smile off my face as I searched the final box up here, utterly charmed by my mate and struggling to understand why. She was everything that should have irritated me, too mouthy, too opinionated, too brash and violent and fierce. And yet I loved all those things about her. Loved that she challenged me and gave me shit and matched me in every possible way.

"Can I touch this?" she asked as I jumped off the chair. She pointed to a bronze compass in dire need of polishing.

"If you want to grow metal spikes all over your body," I replied with a smirk.

"Pass."

I watched her survey the room, greed entering her eyes. Gods, we were so alike. I felt the same way when I was in here. I wanted all of it. I wanted more. More power, more weapons, more magic that could, in untested theory, give me an edge if Cronus ever challenged me. I should have known he never would, should have known he'd wipe me out of existence and save himself the trouble of a fight.

Haley reached towards a jar with a red leaf cutting inside it, its purple veins glowing in a pulse that made it seem alive. I snuck my arm around her waist and pulled her back against me, a metaphorical fist driving into my stomach at the feel of her against me.

I nearly lost her. I nearly fucking lost her.

"I wasn't gonna touch it," she muttered, surly.

I smirked. "Sure you weren't."

I ducked my head and dragged a deep breath into my lungs, her scent of orchids and blood filling my senses until my chest threatened to cave in. I'd really believed the pearl had failed, that she'd been ripped away forever.

"Are you sniffing my hair?" she asked.

I scoffed. "You're delusional."

I expected her to keep teasing me, but instead she said, "Wynvail, you're not a thing, and you have no master. Stop calling yourself shit like that; it's not true, and I don't like it."

I paused, my hand spread across her stomach. "Why?"

She turned, my palm skimming her side until it settled at the small of her back. I flexed my hand, liking touching her like this. Touching Halwen was as dangerous as collecting powerful objects; I always wanted more.

"You're my mate, Wyn," she said, her voice hardening— until my eyes fluttered and I sucked in a breath before I could take control of it. "What?" she breathed, settling her arms around my waist, fingers linked behind my back.

"The first time you called me that," I said, glancing at the shelves and cabinets instead of looking her in the eye, "it felt like I'd won. You believed the fake shit I sold you, and accepted me as your mate, but you only called me that because you thought we'd lived a whole life together. By the time I started giving a damn about you—"

"What?" she pressed, her eyes rapt on my face, almost hungry for every word I spoke.

"Well, you hated me at that point. You saw me for the poison I really am, and I took every insult you threw my way as if it was a term of endearment. I wasn't supposed to care about you."

"You care about me?" she murmured, a deep furrow of genuine confusion between her brows.

"I'm thoroughly enamoured with you, you idiot," I replied,

irritated she didn't know. "I love you. I have since you fought me in the arena, it just took me a while to realise it. When you almost got crushed by the Labyrinth, I figured it out. When you saved me from that hippocampus, there was no going back. I don't just love you; I'm *in* love with you."

Haley's stormy eyes were wide, fixed on mine with an expression I couldn't read. Was she horrified? "You love me?" she breathed.

I'd said it now; I had to own it, no matter how disgusted she was by my feelings. "I do," I replied, unapologetic.

She dropped her hands from my back and slammed them into my chest, shoving me so hard I knocked into the table behind me. Potion bottles and jars rattled. "You absolute fucking bastard! You—you've known for days and you didn't tell me?"

"Remind me when we had a moment to spare on heartfelt conversations and confessions of love," I drawled, worried I'd picked up that plant because I swore spikes formed all over my heart, pointing inward at the fragile organ.

For a long time, I thought Cronus had made me wrong, formed me so I couldn't feel a single positive emotion, only anger and hatred and resentment. Haley's reaction made me wish he had.

In slow motion, I saw a tall, slim bottle of sapphire liquid roll towards the edge of the table, but I was a little distracted by Haley grabbing a fistful of the black T-shirt I wore and yanking me into a bruising kiss.

I groaned, dragging her against me, tasting her moan when she ground her hips against my cock. I'd been hard since I saw her in the doorway, the bare skin of her thigh a sinful temptation.

"I love you," she gasped between fierce kisses. "I loved you even when I hated you."

I cursed and wrenched her back for a rougher, biting kiss,

owning her with every nip of my teeth, every stroke of my tongue, every bruising press of my lips.

"You're fucking mine," I growled, ducking to grab the backs of her thighs, my eyes nearly rolling back at the feel of her soft, heated skin.

She shuddered, fingers locking behind my neck, her eyes dark and glossy with need. Fuck, she was even more beautiful like this. How was that possible? I'd seen this woman kill and hadn't thought there'd ever be a sexier sight.

"Again," she panted, biting her bottom lip when her pussy settled over my hard cock, only my sweatpants between us.

"You—" I growled, grabbing her ass and squeezing tight enough to leave marks, "Are—" I caught her bottom lip in my teeth, grinding until blood beaded on my tongue, surrounding all my senses until I couldn't hold back a low, vibrating noise. *"Mine."*

She gasped, writhing against me, covering my mouth in demanding kisses. "Wyn."

The next noise I made came from deep in my chest, guttural and raw. I used my grip on her ass to grind her pussy against my cock, leaving a wet patch on my pants that drove me fucking wild. I wanted to be covered in her arousal, wanted to wear her scent so there was no doubt that she was mine and I was hers.

"That name," I told her, "is my ultimate weakness. I'm desperate to hear it from your lips every waking moment. I don't care that you only use it when I'm injured; I'll happily draw blood if it puts that name on your tongue."

Although if I could coax it from her with pleasure, that was even better...

"You're insane," she panted, and jumped, clinging to me when a shatter echoed through the cluttered room.

I sighed. The jar had finally rolled off the table. This was just what I needed when my mate's pussy ached for me, so hot I could feel it through the fabric between us.

"Shit, what was that?" she gasped, her grey-blue eyes wide as she scanned the room—and stiffened when she spied the broken bottle on the floor, a plume of thick sapphire smoke rising from it.

"Ignore it," I commanded, my voice deep and hard in a way I hadn't planned. Haley's eyes returned to me, her pupils dilated. Mouth parted on quick breaths. Beautiful.

"You like being told what to do," I remembered, squeezing her ass. "And if I remember rightly, dirty talk will make that sweet pussy wet for me. But filthy talk makes your cunt *soaked*, isn't that right, honey?"

Her throat bobbed. "No," she lied.

I laughed, glancing down between our bodies, her shirt rucked up so I could see a glimpse of that sinful pussy. I could smell her arousal, soaked into my pants, and my mouth watered.

"So you won't drip all over my pants if I tell you all I've been able to think about for *weeks* is ripping your clothes off, spreading these thighs that are trembling around me, and filling your needy little cunt over and over, until you've come so many times you can't take it anymore?"

"Wyn," she whimpered, breathing faster.

"Hm," I said, kneading the soft flesh of her ass and so turned on that fire ran through my veins. "I think you soaked the fabric all the way through, honey. I bet my cock's covered in your arousal. Is that pussy desperate for me? Does it *ache* for me?"

"Yes," she muttered in a sulky little whine that inflated my ego.

I dragged my lips up her throat, impressing the shape of my smirk on her skin. "I know you're a good girl, Halwen. And good girls beg for what they want, don't they?"

She nodded, fast.

"So tell me what you want. Beg for it."

She squirmed against me. "Touch me, Wyn. Please. I need you to touch me."

I kissed the edge of her jaw, throwing a glare at the corner of the room where the thick blue smoke was resolving into the shape of a man. If he could take a hint, he'd fuck off back into the glass he'd come from.

"Touch you where, honey? That's awfully vague."

She rolled her hips against mine, dragging her pussy down my erection. "Touch my clit. Please."

"Good girl for saying please," I praised her, wondering how the fuck I was going to give my mate what she needed and not drop her on her ass. I tried to block out the magical bastard rising to his feet across the room, and banded my arm across Haley's back, curving my hand around her ass cheek. Fuck, her skin was scorching hot. It was cute as fuck when I finally brushed the pad of my thumb over her clit and magic burned bright red from under her shirt. I loved making her lose control. And hey, if she hit me with that glorious power of hers, at least I'd got to touch her.

I brought my thumb to my mouth and groaned when her sweet, smoky flavour burst across my tongue. "You don't know how many times I've imagined your taste." She whimpered, so I went on. "You're even sweeter than I imagined. I think I'm already addicted to your pussy."

Her throat bobbed, her eyes fixed on me, smoky and dark with desperation. I felt the throb of her need through the bond, and possessiveness tightened my hold on her ass.

"I can feel you," I told her, my lips against her ear and a shiver poised at the base of my spine. "Aching for me. *Throbbing* for me." I replaced my thumb on her clit and circled her swollen bud, nearly losing my goddamn mind when it pulsed against my touch.

She dug her fingernails into my shoulders, her hips bucking in response to the stimulation. Greedy for more gasps and moans from those beautiful lips, I adjusted the angle of my thumb, trying every new spot until she was shuddering in my arms, her gasps changing to deep, throaty moans. The sounds wrapped around my cock like a fist until it jerked against her, drawing out another breathy moan when my cock nudged her pussy at the same time I found another weak spot.

"Wyn," she gasped, squirming, breathing faster.

I shot a glare at the sapphire bastard in the corner when he stepped out of the plume of smoke. I mouthed, *fuck off.* He blinked but said nothing, watching Haley and I too closely for comfort. A deep sound of warning formed in my throat, turning my words into a growl when I asked, "Is this pussy gonna come for me, honey?"

She nodded fast, her eyes screwed shut. "Fuck. Don't stop, please don't stop."

I had no intention of it. I didn't stop until she was a shuddering, twitching mess of pleasure in my arms, and even then I made slow circles on her clit, obsessed with every noise and reaction from her body. She was practically liquid in my arms, so limp with pleasure that I thought she'd fallen asleep for a moment.

She jerked up, snapping her head off my shoulder, when the sapphire bastard stepped forward and in a polite voice, asked, "How can I be of service, sir, madam?"

"What the *fuck?*" Haley screeched, gripping my shoulders. Colour flooded her cheeks, mortification filling her soul. I kissed her shoulder and bared my teeth at the bastard who ruined her afterglow.

I prided myself on being composed and in control, a civilised man, but beast blood ran through my veins, and I was every bit as much a sun soul as Harvey. I wanted to rip this fucker's eyes out for looking at her, wanted to sever his tongue for daring to address her. But he wasn't even alive; he was a bit of sentient magic created only to grant wishes.

"Get the fuck out," I growled. "Go back to your damn jar."

"Jar..." Haley murmured, glancing at the shattered glass and putting two and two together. "Who keeps a blue guy in a jar in their house?"

I did. Because there was a chance I could ask this blue guy to find a weakness in Cronus and it might work. Might. But I had more important things on my mind right now. Haley dripped all over my fingers and my arm was going to give out at any moment.

"My jar appears to have broken," the sapphire fucker said, taking another step forward with an amiable smile. "Do you need another participant? I'm well versed in demon sex and female climaxes."

Rage erupted through me, far stronger than the irritation, swallowing even my aching need to be inside her. A deep, animal sound came from my throat, fury twisting my face, curling my upper lip, and I slowly glided my hand from Haley's pussy and grabbed a fistful of magic.

"Wyn, who the fuck is this?" she asked, somewhere between freaked out and pissed off. I barely heard her, blood whooshing in my ears.

I flicked my hand at the sapphire asshole and satisfaction filled my chest to bursting at the bullet of pure silver that shot through the air and buried itself in his forehead. Beings of magic could rarely be killed by any ordinary method, but they were susceptible to magic. I should know.

He staggered back, hands reaching for his head, but his body fell apart before he could touch the hole I blew in his head. First, he became smoke and then even that filtered away.

Haley shuddered in my arms, breathing rapidly again.

"Haley…" I murmured, dragging my attention back to her —and blinking at the frantic desperation tightening her face, widening her eyes.

She shuddered, arching against me, and I remembered, "Violence turns you on."

"I need you," she blurted, sliding her hands into my hair and gripping so tight that sensation shot down my spine and sank into my balls, a groan torn from my lips. "Wyn, please, fuck that guy whoever he was, I *need* you—"

She reached between us and grabbed my cock through my sweatpants and my eyes rolled back, undermining every dominant move I'd made with her tonight. Or ever. She reduced me to a needy fucking virgin, and I couldn't breathe.[1]

"Haley," I warned.

"It's the first time you've called me that," she pointed out, her lips parted and needy fingers pushing down the waist-band of my pants. I grabbed her ass in both hands when her desperate movements threatened to drop her to the floor. "You only called me Halwen before."

"Trying to keep my distance," I replied, and bit the inside of my cheek when her hand gripped my bare cock, the pressure absolutely fucking perfect. A gruff sound caught in my throat, and punched out of me when she stroked me from root to tip.

"But you're not trying anymore?" she murmured.

"No idea what you just said," I bit out, my jaw clenched. My nostrils flared. Fuck. I wouldn't survive this. "Fuck, honey, you need to lighten your grip."

"You like it gentle?" she asked, peering into my face. I wasn't sure what she saw, but it made possessiveness flare through her soul, enflaming my own.

"No," I bit out. "I need to be inside you. Now."

I set her on the floor and ignored the flip-flop of my heart when she pouted. I shoved off my sweatpants, snatched the shirt up over her head and grabbed her again. Her arms wrapped around my shoulders, her legs around my waist. My cock was so close to her pussy, her heat making my eyes roll back. She watched it happen and I could do nothing to hide it. But maybe it was okay to show weakness to my mate.

I tried not to think about the searing heat of her gliding over my cock as I walked us out of the room, kicking it shut behind us. I waited a single millisecond for the shields to kick in and hide it from discovery before I strode down the hallway, throwing open the door of the nearest room. We rarely used this sitting room, preferring the other upstairs, but the only thing that mattered was the sofa five steps in front of me.

I laid my mate out on the flocked red fabric and groaned at the sight of her, flushed with need, completely naked, scarred and tattooed and absolutely fucking gorgeous. There was a freckle on her hip that I was instantly enamoured with; I crawled on top of her, intent on kissing it, but she sucked in a sharp, pained breath and I sat back.

"What?" I demanded, scanning her face, her body. She wasn't bleeding, wasn't hurt that I could see. But this gasp was entirely different to the needy ones from before.

My gut clenched when she sat up. She was rejecting me. Of course she was; she was a goddamn angel, and I was a monster.

"Wyn," she breathed, and—

And reached out to trace the magic branded into my thighs. Ah. Fuck.

"What is this? Who did this?"

I swallowed, ice dumped metaphorically over me. "I'll give you one guess."

Rage exploded through my soul, bleeding out of her so rapidly I expected her to start—glowing. Yup, both curse marks on her arm and stomach blazed to life, matching the fury in her expression.

"Calm down," I murmured, stroking the outside of her

thighs and sitting back on my heels between them. "It's fine; I grew used to the brands years ago. I only notice them when I'm close to him."

"Brands," she whispered, her chest rising and falling fast. I blinked, and I could have sworn her whole body glowed with marks, each one so similar to her curses. But then I blinked again, and it was gone. "He *branded* you?" she snarled, her teeth bared. "He branded my mate?"

"Long before we met," I said, trying to appease her fury. "He did this the day he made me; it was so long ago it doesn't—"

She trembled under me, a constant growl in the back of her throat. "Don't you dare say it doesn't matter."

I shrugged. "It doesn't. This happened a century ago, and most days they don't even hurt—"

"They hurt?" she breathed, her expression frozen.

So obviously that was the wrong thing to say. I didn't know how to calm her, had never seen anyone murderous on my behalf before.

"Do they hurt right now?"

"Only because I'm thinking about them," I answered honestly, ignoring the bite of heat and pain wrapped around my thighs, reminding me of how it felt to kneel on the cold marble floor in front of my creator, my master. Remembering the fire and screaming and the stench of charred flesh as he burned them into my newborn skin.

"You need to stop thinking," Haley said in a calm voice that told me she was anything but. It was a calm that killed people, and I swallowed, flicking my tongue over my dry bottom lip.

"I—" I cut off when Haley pushed me off her.

Shit. Okay. I could accept this, I could swallow the rejection. It was fine. It fucking hurt, far worse than the brands, but it was fine.

Fully intending to go and get dressed and leave her alone

for the rest of my life, I didn't resist her pushing me. My self-esteem had gone from a hundred to zero.

But Haley kept pushing me until I fell against the opposite arm of the sofa, my legs trapped awkwardly under me. By the time I'd pulled them out from under me, she had climbed on top of me and sank halfway down my cock.

Heat. Liquid. Heaven.

I threw my head back and groaned, deep from my chest. My hips bucked without my command, driving me all the way inside her, and my eyes rolled. Oh, fuck. Oh, gods. I panted, breathing fast.

I was shaking when she pulled my head up and kissed me, both fierce and careful at the same time, her hips making slow, small movements that should have made it easier to control my cock's throbbing but somehow didn't.

"Haley," I groaned, heaving for breath like I'd run a marathon. I slammed my hips up again and watched her mouth fall open. "Beautiful, honey, I'm not gonna last."

"I don't care," she replied, some of that rage oozing from her soul into her voice when she added, "Tell me if I hurt you."

"I wouldn't stop you if you killed me," I replied honestly, gripping her hips as she slid up and down my cock, the friction and searing heat making my skin tight over my bones. When she rippled around me, I bit my bottom lip, gripping her hips tighter.

She began to pant as she rode me, and my eyes hungrily devoured every sign of her pleasure—eyelids heavy over her smoky eyes, her mouth parted, a flush moving down her neck to her chest, her movements faster, sharper, desperate.

I couldn't take her lips not being on mine a moment longer; I grabbed rough hold of her hair and dragged her mouth to mine, sucking her tongue the second she opened for me. Her soft cry tasted like pure victory and blinding relief.

She was mine; she wanted me. She wasn't rejecting me. She was *claiming* me.

I went weak when she fought for control of our kiss, teeth snaring my bottom lip and pressing indentations into me. A desperate sound formed in my chest, and I managed to trap it there until she drew blood. Fuck.

"You're mine, Wynvail. No one gets to hurt what's mine."

My breathing cut out for a second. My cock went fucking wild inside her, pleasure boiling in my balls until I was pretty sure my eyes crossed.

"Haley. Shit. I'm so close, I can't—"

She was ruining me. Killing me. And I loved every second.

My whole body tightened, everything so much more intense than when I touched myself. Fucking hell.

"Say it," she ordered, somehow stealing control from me. I shook.

"I'm yours," I panted, digging my nails into her hip, pulling her hair to haul her back to my lips. I needed to kiss her. I needed to own her. I needed her to own *me*.

I forgot she could feel my frantic desperation through the bond until she pressed her chest to mine, her skin scalding, boobs so fucking soft, heart beating so hard I felt it against my own. Fuck, she was burning up, and her hips moved faster, slamming into mine.

"I know," she soothed, fingers stroking through my hair, scraping my scalp until my back arched. "I know you need to come, Wyn. Stop fighting it."

"Oh shit."

My whole body strained against her, and I locked my arms around her back, keeping her flush to me as pleasure clawed itself through my body. The next time she dropped her ass against my hips, her pussy gripped me all the way to the hilt, a choked sound ripped from my chest, and I came so hard my face went numb.

Her high, breathy cry was my only warning before she found her own release, and this time I really did go cross eyed when her pussy clenched around me. She squeezed me over and over until I could do nothing to fight it, and I just kept coming, filling her to the brim and giving her more cum when it spilled out of her.

My legs shook, and that might have been embarrassing if little twitches didn't run through Haley, too, her pussy clamping down around me with every tremor through her body.

"Fuck," she grunted, squirming on my lap when I throbbed inside her, a last drop of cum squeezed from me. "I can—oh god, I can feel your orgasm. It's killing me, Wyn."

"Likewise, honey," I panted, gripping her tighter, pressing her closer. I could only breathe again when her pussy stopped fluttering around me, my climax leaving me limp and weak. I rested my head against the sofa arm and groaned. "Shit, Haley."

She laughed. Cruel minx.

"You like ruining me, do you?"

She propped herself up on my chest and fluttered her eyelashes at me. "Maybe."

Her lips feathered across my throat and under my chin, and a long breath slipped from me, stealing all the stress from my body, soothing my fight or flight instincts for the first time in ... I wasn't sure how long. Maybe my entire existence. Had I ever felt at peace before?

"My temperature's dropping," she murmured, a bright flash of shock and disbelief going through the bond.

"Mm?"

"Wane thinks—" She shook her head, sitting back but not lifting herself from my cock. Keeping us connected. My heart fluttered. "It's crazy, but he thinks I'm—" She bit her lips.

"Thinks what?" I coaxed, trailing soft touches along her thighs.

"He thinks I'm—in a mating cycle."

I blinked.

"And maybe that's why I can't have kids," she added, pain furrowing her brow.

My chest tightened. "You can't have children?" I breathed, sympathy swallowing my heart whole. "Oh, honey. Fuck, I'm so sorry."

She shook her head, her pink hair completely rumpled by my fingers. "It's fine. It doesn't bother me."

I raised an eyebrow. "Like the brands don't bother me?"

"So you admit it!" She pointed at me in an *aha!* moment, like she'd caught me out. "This was all part of my genius plan to get you to confess."

"Mhmm. Sure it was. Back to the mating cycle. You've been hotter than usual?"

"I'm always hot," she quipped, a tooth poking free in a grin. When I kept my eyebrow raised, she huffed. "Fine. I've been hotter than normal, and—so fucking horny. It's crazy. Aphrodite locked us up, we were literally in prison, and all I could think of was cock—"

"Aphrodite *locked you up?*"

Haley winced. "Yeah…"

Emlyn had done his best catching me up on what I'd missed, but he forgot to mention *why* they'd been in Olympus.

"She's dead," I reminded myself, mourning the loss of my peace and breathing deep and slowly to manage my rage. "She's dead, and she deserves it, and—" I paused, giving my mate a wide-eyed look when I realised what she was telling me. "Did I just breed you?"

Her face went scarlet. Even her ears turned red. Cute. She shrugged, silent.

A dark satisfaction uncurled through my chest, primal and

deep. I wasn't responsible for the low sound that escaped me when I guided her onto her back on the cushions, withdrawing my hips a few inches before driving back inside, as hard as fucking diamond.

"Let's make sure, shall we?" I asked, my voice rough, carnal. "Just in case the first time didn't work. Three more rounds ought to do it."

Her stormy eyes flew wide. "Three? I don't think—"

"You can handle it," I purred, snapping my hips into hers and glad I came so quickly. I could fill her with cum over and over, until her womb was full of it. "You're my good girl, aren't you?"

Her pupils dilated. I grinned and kissed her as I thrust balls deep.

I meant what I told her before. I wouldn't stop until she begged me to. The first time she'd been in control, but now? I was taking charge.

CHAPTER 12

HALWEN

*M*y legs wouldn't stop shaking. My pussy was still fluttering, but not with an orgasm —*another* orgasm—simply recovering from getting the absolute life pounded out of it.

Wynvail was insane. He recovered so damn fast between climaxes; the last time he didn't even pull out of me, just coaxed an orgasm from my clit before he began fucking me again, pumping me full of so much cum that we'd completely ruined the sofa. It was beyond a deep clean at this point; it would need to be thrown away and replaced.

I cast a look around the room as I stood, my heart all soft and squishy. "Did you really decorate this place for me? Every single piece of furniture?"

"Every single piece," he agreed, his eyes on the trail of cum running down my thigh, eyes almost black, utterly feral. If I didn't know his cock was too sensitive for me, I wouldn't trust him not to fuck me again. And that dark look was doing things to me—both to my pussy and my belly. They were full of butterflies.

"I love everything in this house," I told him. "Every single thing. You stalked me, didn't you?"

"In every possible way," he agreed, getting to his feet in a fluid, feline movement. "I had to make sure it was right for you. It needed to be perfect."

"It is," I said, fighting a smile. "You're way over the top, and completely unhinged, but—thank you. It really feels like home."

He tugged his sweatpants back on, not knowing how goddamn hot he looked in them, especially shirtless, and wrapped his arms around me from behind. The butterflies in my stomach fluttered when he kissed my shoulder, chaste and sweet.

"That's all I wanted. For you to have somewhere safe that felt like home."

"Even before you fell for me?" I asked, glancing out the window and trying not to notice that it was full dark, not even streetlamps casting a golden glow through the night.

"I was obsessed with you from the first meeting. I wanted you. Needed you with a force I wasn't used to. I knew the house would help me keep you. And at the time, I was hoping the shields would keep your other mates out." He huffed. "Now, we're living with them. Strange how priorities change."

Speaking of priorities... I turned to face him, only light from the hallway lining his sharp profile, his messy hair.[1]

"What you did for Wane in the Damned Realm..."

He fixed his jaw. "Yes?"

"Don't you dare do that again."

He jolted, mercury eyes widening. "Excuse me?"

I jabbed his bare chest, trying to shut out memories of how he looked when he came. And failing. Dammit. "You heard me. If you love me at all, you'll never do *anything* like that again."

"You're telling me not to save your mates again?" He looked entirely baffled, and that made me angrier. Made me sad, too, the emotions conflicting in my chest.

"I'm telling you not to sacrifice yourself again!" I shook my head when he still didn't get it. "The shit you said to me before you—before—" My inhale hissed through my teeth. "You spoke like Wane mattered, and you didn't. Like no one would give a shit if you died. Like no one would miss you."

He glanced away and said nothing, eyes snagging on the darkness outside.

"Well, someone did," I said fiercely. "You matter *to me*, and the thought of losing you again makes me want to massacre my way through the city."

His stare snapped to me, surprise blooming across his face.

"You have a mate, and now you have a *family*. The guys, Verena, me—we're your family. You don't get to do stupid, reckless shit without talking about it first. That's not a request, that's an order."

I shook my head, all the panic and grief of losing him clawing its way through my chest. It had been days since I saw him healed, alive, in Olympus. *Days.* The emotions were still as sharp as razors, cutting my heart and soul to shreds. All my anger and pain and bitter, bubbling hurt came out.

"You didn't even *contemplate* telling us. You knew stepping over that threshold would kill you, knew Cronus would unmake you, and you didn't tell us. We could have figured something out, could have found something to mess with the magic so we could all get out. Hell, I'd have moved back into that place forever if it kept you alive. I can't—describe how it felt to watch you die, to feel—feel you die in the bond. My whole soul went numb and icy, and you just—weren't there. I never, *never* want to feel that again. Not for a single damn second."

I swallowed the knot in my throat, my chest heaving. He was silent, just letting me rant.

"Okay," he said finally.

My shoulders slumped, the anger abandoning me. "Okay?"

He nodded, skimming a knuckle down my bare side. "Okay. I didn't realise you'd care."

I flinched.

"Not like that," he rushed to say, pulling me closer. "I don't mean that as an insult, honey."

"I'm your mate; how else am I supposed to take it?"

"I'm not used to people caring if I live or die. I've never had that before, and quite frankly, I wasn't aware I had that before Cronus unmade me. I only realised how much you cared when—"

"Yes?"

He sighed, stroking my skin like it was a touchstone keeping him calm. Shadows flickered in his eyes, anguish on his stubbled face. "The queen of hell was there when I was brought back. She told me you were—taking it hard."

"She told you I was a total mess, didn't she?" I drawled.

"Pretty much." He folded me into his arms, my cheek resting on his chest. "And the only thing I could think about was getting back to you because you needed me, but later, when I processed what she told me, it felt … weird. I wasn't expecting to be missed, and the fact that you mourned me made me feel more real than I ever had before."

I blinked fast. "Are you trying to break my heart? Because it's working."

He grinned, crooked and sexy. "Just telling you my sad little sob story. Feel free to comfort me with these."

His hands slid up my sides and around to squeeze my boobs, his skin fiercely hot—not cold, not even remotely dead. He was undeniably, ferociously alive. I smacked his hands away just to watch his smile widen.

"You still haven't promised me not to sacrifice yourself again."

"I swear to you, Halwen, I won't willingly walk into death again," he vowed, letting go of me to put a hand over his heart.[2] "Do you want me to kneel?" he added.

"Yes," I hissed, surprised by how quickly his knee hit the carpet. "Now repeat after me."

He groaned. "Why do I get the sense I'm going to regret this?"

I gave him a hard scowl; he sat back on his heels, his hands behind his back, and gave me an attentive look. "My name is Wynvail," I said, testing his willingness.

"My name is Wynvail," he repeated sceptically, eyelids flat over his eyes.

"And I have an amazing family."

He paused, and then repeated the words.

"I have a mate who loves me."

His eyes flickered. His voice was thick and quiet when he echoed the words back to me.

"And people who'll care if I'm hurt."

"People who'll miss me if I die."

"I am valued, and wanted, and *far* from nothing."

He licked his lips, struggling on the last part, so I knelt in front of him, stroking his shoulders, up and down, up and down, my touches soft.

"And far from nothing," he finished.

"I'm not a monster," I said quietly, holding his stare, "or an abomination."

He blew out a rough breath, eyes rising to the ceiling. "Haley..."

"It's true," I swore. "Every word."

He laughed, his expression twisted. "The things I've done—"

"Yeah, and?" I cut him off before he could finish. "You don't know even half of what I've done, and don't get me started on the guys. You're not a monster, Wyn. You're not a bad person."

He shook his head, sneering at the ceiling. "I'm not a good person, Halwen."

"No," I agreed, earning a surprised look. "Just an asshole with a heart of gold. Like the rest of us." I kissed him, sweet but long, lingering until the harsh lines of his body softened.

"An asshole with a heart of gold," he murmured, amusement and refusal both in his eyes.

"You came to the caves when we were going to die. You saved Harvey and Emlyn and got us out of there. You helped keep all of us alive in the Labyrinth, and you almost died fighting shoulder to shoulder with Em. You led us to Wane and helped us save him. And sure, I'm still pissed that you thought you were worthless, so you accepted your death without fighting, *but* what you did was a good thing. Stupid, reckless, imbecilic—"

"Yeah, alright," he huffed, scowling.

"But you let yourself be killed for me, and for Wane. So yeah, you have a heart of gold."

"What about brass?"

My gaze flattened.

"Brass is very fetching."

"Accept that it's gold, or I'm punching you in the dick."

"You like this dick too much to dare," he taunted.

I leaned forward, my lips so close to his, almost touching when I said, "Try me, Wynvail van Khama."

A shudder went through his soul, and he blinked. "Fine, I have a heart of tarnished, scuffed and dented gold."

I'd take it. That was progress.

"What was that, just then?" I asked, sliding my arms around

his shoulders, the two of us knee to knee on the carpet in the middle of the room.

"Nothing," he replied too fast.

"Wyn."

He groaned. "I should never have told you that name was my weakness." Definitely not. But he made me equally weak when he called me honey; I thought I'd never hear that name again, so it meant the whole damn world. "Fine. I presumed you'd keep calling me Locke."

"That monster fucked you up as badly as he did Wane and Harvey. You're not a monster; *he* is, and you don't deserve to be tarred with the same name."

His throat bobbed. "I like Van Khama."

"Good. It's sticking. Now accept that you're not a monster or an abomination, and we can go snuggle in bed. And I don't have to punch you in the dick."

He snorted, hands skimming my hips. "It's not as easy as that."

"I know. But it's true." I chewed my bottom lip. "If you won't accept that Cronus creating you doesn't make you that A word I hate, then will you accept that being reborn, being saved by Hades and Persephone, erased all that? You're a goddamn miracle, Wyn. A gift."[3]

He sighed, thumbs stroking circles on my hips. "I'm not a monster. Happy?"

"Not until you believe it," I murmured and kissed him. "And the other word?"

He groaned. "Do I have to, honey?"

"Words have power, Wyn. How do you think they burrowed into your head and tricked you into thinking they were true? The more you say something, the more real it becomes. Tell me you're not an abomination."

Gods, I hated saying it. It felt like blood and poison in my mouth. He flinched when Wane called him that in the tunnels, and I hadn't forgotten it. That word was covered in thorns, and they bit deeper into his skin every day. Maybe every minute.

"Only because I can feel how twisted up you are," he muttered, not looking pleased. "I'm not an abomination."

He bit out the word, rage in his voice even as sickly, oily shame pumped into his soul.

"You have nothing to be ashamed of," I breathed. "Certainly not being created. You don't have to keep feeling guilt just for existing. If you want to feel guilty for something, give yourself a hard time for ruining the couch."

He smirked.

"Hey! It's covered in your cum; don't fucking smirk."

His smirk became a grin. Smug bastard.[4] "If you expect me to regret that, you're sorely mistaken."

"Hm." I gave him a fake scowl. "Fine, then you're replacing it—with something you choose *for you.*"

He stiffened.

"This house is full of things for me, Wyn. But I'm not living here alone. I'm with you, and Wane, and Em, and Harvey, and Kai, and Verena. This is long term now; we're staying. So get something for yourself, and make this place yours, too."

"Only if everyone else does," he muttered, but he was agreeing so I kissed his cheek.

"Deal. Can we go shower and sleep now?"

He gave me a slow, sweeping stare. "I'm not sure, honey. I'm quite attached to you covered in my scent, my cum. My mark."

I groaned, ignoring my flushed face. "You overbearing men and your caveman qualities."

He snorted as we got to our feet. "Isn't that your type?"[5]

I let him walk in front of me so I could smack his ass, delighted by the pink impression of my hand that formed. "I need to get my shirt."

"Leave it."

"But I want it," I argued.

He gave me an indulgent look over his shoulder. "Fine, what my spoiled mate wants, she gets."

A light flashed in his eyes, brightening the silver.

"What?" I asked, resting my hand on his waist.

"I remembered where I put the bottle I was looking for." He grinned. "We'll get it when we retrieve your shirt."

"What is it anyway?" I asked, a furrow between my brows as he strode up the hallway, picking up speed like he was excited. If this was a weapon of mass destruction, I swear...

"A potion I found decades ago, probably forty years ago now. If you put the bottle to your ear, you can hear a woman singing. It's supposed to be Aceso, a goddess of curing sickness and healing wounds. I thought it might close Wane's wounds."

I ground to a halt, my eyes stinging and heart melting in my chest.

"What?" Wyn asked, turning to look at me and scratching the back of his neck. "Why are you feeling like that?"

I wrenched him close and kissed him breathless.

"Asshole with a heart of gold," I murmured against his lips.

He groaned. "This proves nothing."

I just smiled and kissed him again.

CHAPTER 13

*T*he sun hadn't risen, and it was already eleven o'clock. I bit my lip as I stared out the kitchen window, barely touching the coffee Wane had made me. We'd had to turn on every lamp and light in the house even though it should have been bright morning outside.

"Still not reopened?" I asked him, leaning against the kitchen island while he sat at it, devouring a full English breakfast with the same ferocity as Em, Kai, and Harvey ate.

"Not yet," he confirmed, and shoved a whole sausage in his mouth.[1] "It doesn't feel like they're going to rip open; it feels ... strange."

"Normal," I corrected him, stroking long hair back from his face and avoiding the jagged stumps where his horns used to be. "Your back's supposed to be like this; it just feels weird because it's not what you're used to."

"Mm," he agreed, and devoured three strips of bacon in less than a second.[2]

"It shouldn't be this dark, should it?" Wane murmured between bites.

"No," I agreed. My stomach twisted when I looked outside.

It looked like it was three a.m. I tried not to think about whose doing it was. "The sun will rise soon. It gets dark in Scotland in winter."

Wane nodded, scooping up scrambled eggs, but I knew he wasn't reassured. I dropped a kiss on his head, squeezed him in a back hug, and stepped back.

"It's suspiciously quiet," I said. "I need to check the guys aren't wrecking this house like they did the last one."

Wane laughed—and hooked me with a fast shadow before I could walk away. He spun on his stool, guiding me to stand between his legs. "You think you can leave without giving me a proper morning kiss?"

"My apologies, zivai," I murmured, pretending to be properly chastised.

His thumb stroked the dip under my bottom lip. "I don't think you're genuinely sorry, Haley."

Fuck. I could not handle that tone of voice without turning a quivering ball of need. I wasn't even overheated this morning. It seemed to make zero difference where my body was concerned.

"The rest of your food is getting cold," I pointed out, a hot throb starting between my legs.

"You think I care about food when you've got that needy look in your eye?"

I scowled. "You *put* that needy look in my eye. Now I know what you can do with your shadows, I can't look at them innocently anymore."

"These shadows?" he asked, something wicked barely hidden behind the neutral expression on his face.

I jumped when pressure grazed my hip bone and slid under the loose grey sweatpants I wore with a white T-shirt.[3] When the shadow tendril wound around my upper thigh, so close to where heat pounded through my clit, I raised an eyebrow at my innocent mate and leaned closer, my arms on either side of him, palms braced on the kitchen island.

"Verena could walk in at any moment," I pointed out, my heart skipping at the dark sheen of lust in Wane's silver eyes.

"Then we'll be quick. And *quiet,* won't we, itzaia?"

He made that difficult when his shadow explored higher, gliding through my wetness and making me very glad I hadn't put on underwear yet. I bit my bottom lip, toes curling inside my fluffy socks when he found the angle on my clit that made everything tighten inside me. I strangled a groan in my throat, but it escaped when Wane surged forward and kissed me. He was rough and possessive, every brush of his lips claiming me as his, every stroke of his tongue reminding me who I belonged to.

He dragged himself away from my mouth to gasp down air, hot breaths meeting my throat before he sucked my skin into his mouth. No doubt leaving a mark. My pussy throbbed, so wet that when his shadows seemed to multiply, one obsessing over that angle on my clit while another brushed my entrance, it was sucked inside by the greedy throbbing of my inner muscles.

I moaned—and shuddered when Wane's hand covered my mouth. My knees went weak.

"Quiet, itzaia," he warned, something brighter in his eyes, a sharp, masculine satisfaction that made it harder to keep quiet. "That's it, Haley, don't make a single noise while my shadows fill your hot, throbbing pussy."

Oh gods, not dirty talk. Please, no. I sank my teeth into my bottom lip, a tremor going through me. His shadow moved sinuously inside me, stroking, massaging, relentless as it fucked me.

Wane set his mouth to my ear, and my eyes damn near rolled back when he said, "My shadow's soaked. Did you need me this badly? Did you need to be stretched around a fat shadow cock? I can't give you my flesh and blood cock when someone could walk in on us, but you love my shadows don't you, my beautiful mate? You're gripping them so tightly; I can feel every clench and shudder in your pussy."

I panted fast, letting go of the counter to grip Wane's waist, digging in my fingers, my whole body tight and shaky. With every word, the shadow cock thickened and grew inside me, moving expertly so it stroked every ruinous spot inside me, knowing exactly how to make my knees buckle. Wane's arm banded across my back, holding me up, not letting me escape his torturous, obsessive ministrations for a second.

When the shadow on my clit stopped moving, I was able to catch my breath—until his hand slid between us and inside my sweatpants, an obscenely wet sound meeting my ears when his fingers glided through my pussy to my clit.

"Fuck," Wane grunted, hauling me closer, trapping his hand and shadow between us. "So wet for me, itzaia. Are you as dripping wet inside?"

My head was starting to spin. I didn't realise what he planned until his fingers slid through my arousal and pressed inside me, curling in a way that made my mouth fall open. The stretch, the wicked, stroking movements of his shadow deep inside me, and now his fingers relentless in search of my g-spot—

I choked on a moan, my hips stuttering as they tried to escape, tried to press him deeper. Fuck, he was—incredible.

When his mouth fastened to my throat, shadows swirling inside me and his thumb finding my clit, a very unattractive gurgling sound left my throat and my hips snapped forward as I came. His shadow moved even faster, and I gripped him so tightly I ripped his shirt, my eyes screwed shut as his fingers sped, the pressure too much, the *pleasure* too much.

I couldn't take it, my hips jerking wildly, pussy so slick that every thrust of his fingers was so loud, and wetness drenched

Wynvail's sweats. For the second time in twelve hours. This time there was more. A lot more.

"Oh fuck," Wane breathed, and then, his voice an octave lower, *"Fuck."*

That deep, raspy voice made me shake harder, pleasure blurring the whole world around me. My cry was barely muffled by his hand. By the time his shadow withdrew, and his fingers stilled, I couldn't remember my own name.

"Did you just make her squirt?" Kai demanded in a hissed whisper. When did Kai get here? I peeled my eyelids apart, but they stayed low over my eyes as I glanced over my shoulder and found him and Wynvail in the doorway.

"I'm gonna need those pants back," Wynvail said, his eyes dark on where—ugh. Where wetness had splashed across the crotch and leg. Wait, did Kai say squirt...? Was that why my climax was so intense I was still shaking? Why I felt like my skeleton was going to vibrate out of my skin?

"When I've washed them," I mumbled, my head kinda spacey.

"No," Wynvail growled, his eyes fixed to the place Wane's hand slid out of my pants, on the barest glimpse of pink skin before he settled the waistband in place. "I want them as they are."

"Mh," I agreed, not really caring.

I leaned into Wane when he wrapped his arms around me, a kiss feathering across my temple. I felt strangely disconnected from my body, but not like when I was dead; more like I'd reached a new stage of enlightenment where I didn't need a body. Fuck, I felt good.

I was vaguely aware of the pure smugness in Wane's soul, the dark possessiveness in Wyn's and the shock bleeding into lust from Kai.

"Damn, Wane," Kai huffed, stealing into my pleasant floatiness when he crossed the kitchen and moulded himself to my back. "No wonder you made her pass out that time."

Wane snorted, but he was pleased. He loved Kai being impressed by him.[4]

"I look like I pissed myself," I mumbled, resting my head on Wane's shoulder and pulling his sweet scent into my lungs.

"I'd still think you were beautiful if you did," he assured me, kissing the side of my head.

"Maybe the kitchen wouldn't be the best place for it," Wynvail drawled, sending a brush down my soul that made me sigh, my eyelids fluttering again. At least until I realised that beneath the lust and envy in Wyn and Kai's souls there was a common thread of unease.

I straightened, forcing my heavy eyelids to fully open, pointedly *not* looking at the dark stain on my stolen sweatpants. "What?" When they were silent, I gave them matching hard looks, the last buzz of my orgasm clearing. "Kai. Wyn. What is it?"

"You're happy right now," Kai sighed, reaching up to graze my jaw with a knuckle. "Don't make me ruin that, my rose."

I felt his stubbornness set in and transferred my stare to Wyn. "If you don't tell me, I'll keep these sweatpants forever. The first thing I'll do is wash them. Twice."

It was insane; this would never work. There's no way he'd care so much about—

"Fine," he muttered, nostrils flaring. "But take them off now and hand them over. We'll exchange goods at the same time. I don't trust you not to renege on the deal. Sorry, honey."

I snorted but stepped away from Wane and shimmied the grey pants down my legs. I blinked when Wyn pulled a newspaper from his back pocket, handed it over in exchange for the pants and—immediately brought them to his nose.

"You are very not normal," I told him, giving him a strange look before I unfolded the paper and—

UK SET FOR TWENTY DAYS OF DARKNESS the headline yelled in bold, black all-caps.

"Abnormal," Wyn corrected, not a single fuck given.

I swallowed, speed-reading the article, my stomach knotting tighter with every word. Wane wrapped his arms tighter around me, gripping a little fiercely as he read over my shoulder.

"Shit," he breathed when he reached the end.

Yeah.

Every weather expert in the country was studying the strange darkness. No one knew the origins. Certainly no one knew it came from a titan with a deadly agenda. Global warming causing strange weather patterns seemed to be the general consensus, which made zero sense. Most experts agreed on one thing: the darkness wasn't going anywhere, and the sun wasn't rising for *weeks*. A shadow had moved across the Earth and blacked out the sun, and my heart beat faster as I realised—it wouldn't end. Cronus would get the power he wanted, he'd take over the world, and there'd never be sunlight ever again.

"Wane," I breathed, turning to wrap my arms and wings around him, my heart breaking.

"It's fine," he insisted, but it wasn't.

He and Harvey had been raised in darkness, never seeing the sun for twenty fucking years. Harvey had been locked in the tunnels of Alphaven for so long that his sun soul twisted into a shadow beast. I swallowed hard, fighting tears of rage. It wasn't okay.

I promised Harvey we were done with gods and battles—and that included revenge, too. It was better to live our whole lives in the dark than live no lives at all.

So I kissed Wane's cheek and swallowed back all the words I wanted to say.

CHAPTER 14

WANE

*T*here was a tight, sick feeling in the pit of my stomach, and it refused to leave. The house blazed with light from two dozen lamps and lights, but the darkness lurked right outside, and every time I looked at it, I was back in the tunnels under the Damned Realm, festering, broken. One time the titan had ordered me to return to my room and forbidden Andryas to guide me through the warren of tunnels. He'd just snapped my horns off, and I could barely move without screaming and wanting to curl into a tight ball. I was forced to crawl the whole way back. That was the first day I wanted to die.

I didn't want to go back there—not just to that putrid room, but to that headspace. I cast a look over Haley—aggressively polishing her knife collection on the sofa, her legs thrown over Kai's lap—and rose from the armchair I'd been sitting in.

I loved my mate more than life itself, but sometimes it was

hard to talk to her without burdening her, too. She had enough stress, even if we were supposed to be, and I quote, *living happily ever after.*

It might have been happy if the world wasn't under complete darkness. Or if we didn't know the titan who made my life a living hell for the last century was behind it. He killed me over and over and over, dragged me back to life as many times, and I couldn't shut down my terror that he'd do it again, and not just to me.

I knew this panic would eat me alive, so I soothed Haley's stab of worry at seeing me leave by telling her I was going to the kitchen for a drink, and instead went in search of Harvey.

I was worried about my brother. He'd been more closed off from me the past three days since Haley came back to life, and I knew it was because his emotions were huge and vicious right now. Mine were, too. If we spoke about them, maybe we could fix it? Or maybe I was a fool. My optimism should have been slaughtered by the titan decades ago, but spending this time with Haley had renewed it, like it had only been hibernating.

Maybe Haley was right and we would live happily ever after. Gods knew we deserved it.

"Harvey?" I asked, pushing open the kitchen door and peering inside. Except for soup bubbling away in a pot, it was empty. I checked the soup wasn't about to burn and left the room, heading upstairs after searching all the rooms on this floor.

I brushed my fingers over the spiral hilt of the dagger Haley gave me, strength infusing me, filling my lungs with air. *You're safe, and I'll always protect you—but you can use the knife to stab your enemies in the throat yourself. You're a badass, too.* She'd never know how important those words were, and how badly I'd needed to hear them.

My head snapped up when quick movement blurred

131

through my peripheral, and my brows slammed down at the sight of Verena sprinting from her room to the bathroom.

"Verena?" I asked, quickening my pace to catch up to the girl.

She didn't stop to glare at me or even give me a sassy look; she darted into the bathroom and slammed the door shut.

"Are you okay?" I called through the door, instantly concerned. Verena was confrontational, not evasive, so something had to be badly wrong.

"Go away," she replied, but her sharp tongue was noticeably absent.

"I'm not going anywhere," I said firmly. "Tell me what's wrong."

If the titan had got to her, I'd kill him. If any one of our family had upset her, I'd give them a black eye.[1]

When Verena said nothing, worry tightened my heart.

"If you tell me, I can help, Verena," I said gently, watching the dark door for any hint that it might open.

"It's none of your business," she muttered. "Go away."

"Do you want me to get Haley?"

"No!" She sounded panicked.

If we weren't still in the awkward getting-used-to-each-other phase, I'd have used a shadow to break the lock and burst inside, but this wasn't Haley. Verena was a teenager, a young girl who barely knew me. Breaking the door would terrify her and I'd seem like a threat. So I hovered outside the door, prepared to stay for as long as it took.

"I'm not going anywhere," I told her, shadows flickering at my shoulders as nerves mounted. "If you don't want me to get Haley, tell me what's wrong."

She let out a throaty growl that I suspected only teenagers could make, equally deep and high pitched. "Fine! I started my period, okay? Are you happy now?"

I exhaled a rough breath, my shoulders slumping. That

was all? "There's a shelf next to the toilet with purple, flowery bags on them." Because Wynvail had unleashed his interior decorating eye even on sanitary products. "Can you see them?"

"Yes," she breathed, relief in her voice until she let out a squeak I suspected I wasn't supposed to hear. "What the fuck is this? This is a goddamn torture device!"

My lips quirked, a smile fighting to come through. "Let me in, Verena. I'll help you find them."

"No," she muttered.

"Do you *need* help?"

There was a long pause, and then she begrudgingly answered, "Yes."

I sent a thin tendril of shadow through the crack between the door and the frame and used it to twist the fancy lock on the doorknob. The best we'd had before was a deadbolt on the bathroom door and it didn't keep any of us out; that had been chaotic as fuck.

I quickly assessed the situation. Verena stood by the window with one of those thin stick things in her hand, her face so pale her freckles stood out darkly.

"You don't have to use them," I assured her, grabbing the other bag and unzipping it. "We have these, too. What do you usually use?"

Verena snatched the plastic-wrapped, modern-day rag out of my hand, clutching it to her chest. The tips of her ears turned pink, her eyes shifting around the room, not meeting mine. "I don't," she bit out.

I opened my mouth to tell her it was normal during stressful periods of a woman's life for their period to stop—it had happened to my mate, before we realised her body was trying to establish a heat cycle—but then the penny dropped. It wasn't that being kidnapped by Aphrodite had paused her cycles; this was her first one.

"I'm not the most informed person to help with this," I said, trying to catch her gaze. She avoided my attempts. "The last time Haley had a period, it was a hundred years ago and all she had to use were rags."

Verena wrinkled her nose. "Rags?"

"It's exactly what it sounds like. Strips of fabric to line underwear."

"I can't believe I'm having this conversation with you," she muttered, throwing a quick scowl at me.

"Why? There's nothing wrong with a period, Verena." Haley had taught me that lesson swiftly when I turned my nose up at the sight of blood on her smallclothes. She kneed me in the dick and then gave me a two-hour lecture. I repeated it to Verena now, albeit abbreviated. "It's a completely natural thing, and there's no reason to be ashamed of it or to keep it secret."

She rolled her eyes. "Men can't handle periods. Everyone knows that."

"Boys can't," I corrected. "Men have grown up and they know better. If the stick scares you, use the folded thing."

The world had changed a lot since I was last alive; I had no idea what to call most things that existed now. Curiosity was the only reason I knew what was in the zippered bags at all. That, and Kai thought Wynvail was hiding snacks in them because the packaging rustled. Moron.

Verena clenched her jaw and thrust the bag of sticks at me. I closed it and put it back on the shelf, wondering if Wynvail might have been a better person to advise her. He obviously knew enough about these to buy them. But Wynvail wasn't here; I was.

Verena muttered something too quiet for me to hear.

"What? You don't need to whisper, Verena; there's no shame in having a period."

"Fuck, this is mortifying. I hate you."

I just smiled, waiting patiently until she exploded, "I don't know how to use this!"

I wanted to hug her, but I'd probably be crossing lines since we were still close to strangers. I'd hugged her once, but only because we were all grieving Haley. I was extremely conscious that I was a grown man, an adult, and she was a kid. Just the idea of anyone taking advantage of her made me want to shatter the whole world from under us. That might have been an extreme reaction; I'd been locked up for a hundred years, I couldn't tell.

"That's okay," I soothed. "I bet Haley didn't have a clue the first time she saw one." Actually, she'd been in a heat cycle the whole time we'd been resurrected so... "She probably still doesn't. Open it up; there might be instructions."

There weren't instructions, but it seemed self-explanatory. "Like a rag," I murmured. "It probably just sits in your under-wear. The flaps must wrap arou—"

"Okay, out!" she snarled, only meeting my eyes to glare with the force of a thousand burning, embarrassed suns. "Get the fuck out! I'll figure it out myself. And don't *ever* use the word flaps in my presence again."

I allowed her to push me out of the bathroom, a strange smile trying to form on my face. I'd given up on being a father decades ago, but this felt pretty close. It felt ... good to help her. To do something useful that wasn't using my shadows to attack someone. Violence was a useful tool, but it wasn't all I was. I wanted to help too, and even though Verena slammed the door on my face and snapped the lock back into place, I got the sense I *had* helped her.

And strangely, I didn't feel the sharp edge of panic biting into my soul anymore. Helping her had settled me.

So I returned to the living room and plopped back into the chair, my heart going soft when I saw Haley asleep on the sofa, two knives clutched to her chest like a teddy bear.

I said nothing when Verena stalked into the room ten minutes later and thrust a cup of tea at me, but I couldn't stop my smile at the obvious *thank you* gesture. She didn't speak a single word, just went to sit in the window seat and stare into the darkness outside, but the drink meant far more than I could ever put into words. I swore my heart warmed by degrees as I drank it, like she'd infused it with magic and care.

I'd finally relaxed, my body weight sinking into the cushions and my chest opening up to air, when a fist hammered on the front door downstairs.

Haley jerked upright, knives pointed outward. Kai leapt off the sofa with a snarl.

"No one's supposed to be able to find the house, right?" I asked, all my calm vanishing, replaced by spiky panic.

"No," Haley snarled, stalking across the rug, "They're not."

Which meant only one thing—the shields had broken.

CHAPTER 15

HALWEN

"There's no back door?" I demanded, my heart thumping faster. "What good is a safe house without a second exit?"

"It's an oversight I'll correct as soon as we kill the threat at the front door," Wynvail assured me calmly, standing straight-backed at my side with moonlight pooled in his hand.

Kai and Em were a solid wall of protective menace at my back, and Harvey shielded behind them with Verena who refused to stay behind. Wane had thrown up a wall of shadows in front of me, his whole body trembling. I reached out to his soul, hating the way he rebuilt his walls higher every day. I was glad he was healing from his ordeal, but I worried he was trying to hide his suffering from me. Visions flashed behind my eyes of Andryas Revairs hacking off his wings, and the anger that rose gave me the last oomph to reach for the door.

I threw it open, Wane's shadows snapping through the gap

and grabbing the hooded figure standing on the doorstep. They were barely visible in the pitch blackness, just a shape of a person.

"Wait!" I gasped when I glimpsed a purple hand as she struggled against his shadows, sharp black hair flicking out from within the hood. "Stop! It's my friend. It's Renna!"

A quiet voice in my head breathed, *thank fuck.*

I'd missed my friends. I needed someone to talk to, to blurt all my emotions out to, to listen and judge and then advise me. I'd always honour my promise to Harvey to stay away from anything that would put us at risk, but when Renna literally landed on our doorstep ... I could hardly turn her away. That was just bad hospitality.

"How the fuck did you find me?" I demanded, grabbing her arm. "We're supposed to be hidden."

And that was worrying as fuck. If Renna could track us down, Cronus would have no trouble doing the same. Or would he send his cronies instead? Even now I couldn't get Iapetus's threats out of my head, his horrible, oozing suggestions. That voice had sunk into my head and even death wouldn't dislodge it.

"Did you use the tracking stone?" Kai asked, less hostile than he'd been seconds ago. Huh. I guess he and Renna were more frenemies than enemies after Olympus.

"Yes," Renna agreed, lowering her hood. "It led me here."

"It led me here," I parroted in the same robotic voice. "What are you being so serious for?"

She hadn't sworn or insulted me yet, hadn't threatened me or whipped out a weapon.[1]

"You snake cocksucking bitch!" a high, raspy voice yelled, so loud it filled the whole street.

Wane darted past me, staring up the road. "I don't know who that is."

"That's not Renna!" the woman screamed, and I was so

paranoid I didn't even question it. When Renna backed up a step, I lashed my hand out and snatched her wrist, yanking her back up.

"Wane, bind her," I growled, my heartbeats coming faster, rage pumping through me with each one.

"She's lying," Renna argued, looking me right in the eye. "Why are you doing this?"

"Not a single curse spat at me?" I scoffed. "As if you're Renna."

The seething, spitting-mad woman racing down the street was Asta, her grey hair unbraided and loose, a wild halo around her aged face. Rage was emblazoned on every one of her features, her sharp teeth bared, and the air crackled with danger around her—and extremely powerful magic.

My own power responded, blood magic leaping to life for the first time since I died. The rapid thumps of my family's hearts filled my ears, Verena's a frantic *thud-thud*, standing out among them all. Asta's heart beat erratically, drawing my attention and making Renna's slow, even thump even more obvious.

"You're fucking dead!" Asta screamed, reaching the house and practically vaulting the gate, her grey lips pulled back from her teeth and her nostrils flaring. "Where's my wife?"

I sucked in a sharp breath. "Wait. She took Renna?"

"*He* took Renna," Asta growled, her voice deeper, richer. "Cronus." She spat on the path.[2]

"Shit," I breathed, my stomach twisting up tight. Cronus had Renna.

"And he replaced her with this fake fucking clone, like I wouldn't recognise my own *wife* was missing," Asta went on, her face a grotesque mask of fury.

"She's a made thing, like me," Wynvail said, his irritation about the path vanishing. I reached behind myself and grabbed his hand, squeezing tight.

"You're not a thing," Harvey argued before I could, and I fell even deeper in love with him for his protectiveness.

"Tell me where she is," Asta growled, spinning the fake Renna around and ripping her hood off her face. She was still bound in Wane's shadows; she couldn't go anywhere to escape Asta's wrath. *"Where is my wife?"*

Sympathy bled through my soul, my mates recognising her panic, knowing it intimately. I knew it, too, and wished I didn't.

We were supposed to be staying safe, staying out of trouble. But fuck, when it turned up on the doorstep what were we supposed to do?

Emlyn brushed past me onto the top step, his jaw clenched and anger written in the lines on his forehead. "Answer her," he ordered the fake Renna. "Or you'll have all of us to answer to."

Fake Renna shook her head, dark hair swinging.

Asta unleashed a dark and throaty hiss, and magic rattled the air as she shoved her hand at Fake Renna's chest. No *into* her chest. She grabbed her heart, ripped it out, and crushed it into dust in the same second. I swallowed, watching it collapse into nothing, and then Renna's body disintegrated in front of me, too.

I backed up a step, my stomach trying out a convincing washing machine impression. She turned to ash. Disintegrated.

Unmade.

Wyn tightened his hand around mine, but it wasn't enough. Emlyn and Wane were ahead of us; I trusted them with my back, so I turned and buried my head in Wyn's chest, dragging his scent into my lungs, surrounding myself with him.

"I'm fine, honey," he promised, kissing my hair as I shook, trapped in that moment, the memory cruelly clear. He was heavy in my arms, cold leaching through the bond, my soul so numb as death stole him from me. And then I was covered in ashes—and then nothing. No sign that he'd ever lived.

"I'm right here, Haley," he murmured, lips brushing the shell of my ear. "You can feel me; you can hear me. I'm not going anywhere, either. I'm far too obsessed with you to leave for more than a few minutes at a time."

A smile tried to form on my face, but it was too soon. Too soon after he died, and after I came back from death. Kai and Harvey pressed in around me, soothing with their touches, and I wrangled my composure with effort. I expected Asta to be staring at me, confused, but she just snarled at the step where Fake Renna had stood, breathing hard, her teeth still bared.

I dragged my stare to Wynvail and looked deep into his eyes, reaching for his soul to reassure myself he was okay. He wasn't even in pain, wasn't stressed—just worried.

"Asta," I said, gentling my voice. "Do you want to come inside?"

She inhaled a shuddering breath and clenched her jaw. When she met my gaze, it wasn't rage burning in her eyes but devastation.

I stepped out of the warmth of my mates and opened my arms, expecting her to sneer, but she fell into me and clung hard. Fuck.

Renna was really missing.

And if a fake impostor had managed to find us, it meant our shields were screwed.

"Wane, Wynvail, renew the wards," Emlyn quietly ordered, following my line of thought. "Hales, take Asta into the living room. I'll make tea."

CHAPTER 16

*A*sta's hands shook as she brought the cup of tea to her lips, making a face when she took a sip. "Sugar?"

"For shock," Emlyn explained in his softest voice. His compassion was every bit as vast and all-consuming as his protectiveness, and my heart melted.

Asta nodded and swallowed. "After Olympus, and all that bowing bullshit ... I couldn't find her. And then she came home yesterday and started acting weird, asking too many questions about you, pressing for where we'd hidden you. Cronus thinks Hell is shielding you. Like we're not a complete fucking shambles," she laughed bitterly.

I reached out to squeeze her hand, at a loss for what to say.

"Lucifer is gone," she muttered. "Lili and the guys are a fucking mess. Tali's rampaging her way through the realm, grieving two of her best friends."

"Two?" I asked, my heart hurting for all of them. I squeezed Asta's hand, wishing I could help. Knowing I couldn't.

"Luc and you," Asta muttered, like I was an idiot for not figuring that out. "Last I saw her, she was ripping the head off a rebel. Good for her," she added, swallowing a gulp of tea. "You could have put brandy in this. Just saying."

"If he wants to use Renna against Haley, she'll still be alive," Wynvail said carefully, watching Asta. "He won't kill her."

"Yet," she laughed, a low, twisted thing. She glanced at all of us. "Come back with me. We've got the spirits under control now, and Iarlon is stable even if the rest of the realm is a bloodbath. Lili needs a friend, and I'm no fucking help. The ruling circle can't afford to fall apart right now; everyone's looking for a weakness to exploit. But five archdemons and—whatever the hell you are," she said to Wynvail, "it would make a difference. Appearances are everything."

"He's mine," I said coldly. "That's what he is."

Wynvail had clenched his jaw, but he shot me an adoring look now, softening.

"And," I sighed, releasing her hand, cold spreading through me, "I'm sorry, Asta. We've died too many times; I only just came back. I can't walk into danger again. I'll do whatever I can to help you find Renna, but I can only help from here. I can't come with you. I'm sorry," I repeated when she threw me a disgusted look.

"My wife is missing and—"

"My mate *died*," Kai cut her off, his voice lethal. "Are you asking her to die again so we can save the woman you love? Will you play god, letting my mate die to save yours?"

"No," Asta snarled, teeth bared again. She slammed her mug down on the coffee table. "I'm asking for your *help* but fuck you. Fuck all of you."

"I can't do it to them again," I choked out, feeling like total shit. "I'm sorry Asta. I really am."

"Some friend you are," she spat, getting to her feet. "Do you think staying here will keep you safe? Do you think Cronus won't find you? Renna's doppelganger found you; I followed her, I didn't lead her here. She *knew* where you were. Cronus will find you, like he'll find *all* of us, and—"

"I'd appreciate it," I bit out, shoving off the sofa and aware my whole body was bristling, "if you didn't say this in front of our thirteen-year-old. *Thanks*," I added, probably a little too bitchy.

Asta seemed to notice Verena for the first time and deflated. "Fine," she said under her breath. "I'll find Renna myself."

"I have something you can use," Wynvail offered, following her out the door.

"Keep it. I don't need anything from you bastards."

She didn't stick around long enough for Wynvail to give her anything; her boots thundered out the living room and down the stairs. The door slammed downstairs; I listened for the sound of the locks falling into place and Wyn's steps coming back up to us and scrubbed my face.

Fuck.

Just ... fuck.

CHAPTER 17

EMLYN

One look at my mate, and I knew what thoughts spun around her head, tormenting her. She was supposed to be throwing knives at the dummy in the middle of the training room, but she'd been holding this knife for at least a minute, her eyes unfocused.

I sighed, unwrapping the boxing gloves from my hands with my teeth and dropping them onto a table so I could wind my arms around my mate's waist.

She'd tried to insist on alone time, but I knew her better than I knew myself; she was stressing, and stressing led to spiralling, which led to self-destruction. So I dropped a kiss on her shoulder and waited for her to open up. I wasn't going anywhere until she confided in me, and after ten years together (give or take a hundred) she knew that.

"I can't do it, Em," she said after a long silence. Her shoulders slumped; she turned the knife over in her hands. "I'm trying so damn hard for you guys, but I—"

"It's killing you," I finished gently when she faltered. I kissed the side of her neck, a luxury afforded to me by the ponytail she'd put her hair up in. "Your friend's in danger and sitting back and doing nothing isn't in your make-up."

"Yeah," she breathed. "But Harvey and Kai can't handle me getting hurt again, Wyn will completely lose it, and you can pretend everything's fine, but I know you're struggling, Em."

She turned in my arms, fixing me with a concerned look that made my stomach jolt and flutter. She saw right through me, and I could never tell whether to be nervous or touched.

"You can't hold all of us together all the time when *you* need holding together, too," she murmured, brushing the backs of her fingers over my cheek and down my beard. "I love how protective you are, and I love your big heart, but you can't constantly put all of our needs ahead of yours. Forget all of us for a minute; what do you need, Em?"

My first answer was automatic. *I just need you.* But what did I need? Really? I skimmed my hands down her sides, stroking her hips with my thumbs.

I didn't like my answer. It wasn't straightforward, wasn't palatable even to myself. I didn't want to want it, but I sighed and admitted, "I want this to be over, Hales. And it isn't. I *hate* knowing the monster who took you from us is out there, a fucking king taking over the world when he stole my world from me."

My breathing came heavier, faster. Haley slid her fingers into my hair and stroked it as I spoke, words pouring out.

"He could come for us at any moment—Asta was right, we're not safe, we're just lying to ourselves. He's a threat, and our safety is just an illusion."

I didn't dare say this to anyone else, terrified to break that illusion, but Haley would stand right beside me and keep up the pretence to protect the rest of our family.

"So I want him gone. I want him dead, and every threat he

poses wiped out so we don't have to pretend to be safe. I want us to *be* safe."

Her gaze was steady on me, full of understanding and love. It helped me get my breathing under control.

"But I'm not allowed to want that," I murmured, squeezing her hips, "because that puts us back in the same situation where we lost you. There's no guarantee we'd win and kill him. We could lose you again; you could lose us again. We lost once, and chances are too damn high that the same thing will happen again. We're all right on the precipice of a very serious breakdown, and only you coming back to us halted it—but it's one bad event away."

Haley nodded, sadness heavy in her eyes now. They were a storm, those eyes—grey with the barest hint of green and blue, full of clouds and shadows. She'd been through enough. But Cronus could turn up at any minute.

"I understand now," I murmured, bringing a hand to her jaw and tilting her head back, resting my forehead on hers. "Why you couldn't stay in the safe house and wait for the next mercenary to find us. I didn't understand back then, maybe I was more mentally stable a hundred years ago, I don't know."

I expected her to laugh at my sad attempt at a joke, but she just tilted her face forward and kissed me, full of emotion.

Fuck. I swallowed a sudden lump in my throat.

"So what do you want to do, Em?" she asked quietly.

"I don't know what I want," I replied, thick with rage and tears. "But I think what I need is a way to shield us from him. For good."

She drew back a few inches and raised an eyebrow. I was very familiar with that slow arch of judgement.

"What?" I asked, my mouth flickering into a smile.

"That's not what you need, Em. That's what the guys need."

"What I need is to fuck you in every position imaginable," I muttered.

"That can be arranged," she replied with a smile. "But cut the shit, Emlyn Johahn. Tell me."

"I need to watch him die, Hales. I want to see his body explode the way you've killed so many threats to us. I want your magic to cut into every single part of him, and I want you to rip him apart until the whole goddamn world is covered in his blood."

Haley kissed me—slowly, calming the thunderous beat of my heart with every glide of her tongue, every soft press of lips on mine.

"I did try," she said quietly. "It didn't work. But if I ever get another chance—"

I shook my head. "We threw everything at him and none of it worked. We need something new."

A dark gleam flashed in her eyes. "You really mean it. You want us to kill him."

"Before he kills us," I agreed, kissing her, stroking my thumb over her jaw. "It's him or us, Hales. Right now, he doesn't have proof you're alive. But how long until he comes for you? I think you were just another descendant to him before, but now? You fought him—and *survived*. He's going to take that personally."

"I know," she agreed, chewing her lip. "To summarise, we need new, better shields, a way to really, truly kill Cronus, and an uninterrupted afternoon for you to fuck me senseless. Did I forget anything?"

"That's most of it," I murmured, sliding my hand from her hip to her ass, helping myself to a squeeze of softness and muscle.

"Most?" Her brow furrowed, the expression cute as fuck.

I kissed her cheek, my lips brushing a new scar acquired in Olympus. "We need to find your friend and get her to safety. You'll never live with yourself if we don't. And neither will I."

I wasn't prepared for the force of her kiss, or for her

fingers to tighten in my hair, ripping out a few strands.[1] I sighed, melting into her, and slid my hands under her ass to pull her up against me. Teeth caught my bottom lip, dragging a growl from me. It turned into a groan when she wrapped her legs around my hips, wiggling over my cock. I was rock hard the second her pussy settled over me, as hot as a furnace even through our clothes.

I was one second away from exploring one of those many positions we'd spoken about when the room plunged into sudden darkness.

Haley squeaked, pulling me closer and pressing herself against my chest in the same movement.

"Probably just a power cut," I murmured, kissing her cheek.

But when we went downstairs and found the rest of our family, it didn't take longer than two seconds to realise it wasn't a power cut. The lights were still on; the TV was still playing. We just couldn't see them because complete darkness had blanketed the whole house.

CHAPTER 18

HALWEN

"Don't make me regret this," Wynvail muttered, unlocking the shields on his secret armoury and giving the guys—Kai and Verena especially—a warning look. "Don't steal anything, don't touch anything unless you want your dick to shrivel or for you to shift into an armour plated hedgehog."

"Why would you have something that does that anyway?" I asked, giving him a strange look as he led us inside the narrow room.

"Reasons," Wynvail replied, giving me a look that told me he was remembering the last time we were here, and what that led to.

The armoury smelled of herbs and magic, the air biting my skin. The light of Wynvail's silver-white magic made the shelves of bottles, strange objects, and magic shit even more unearthly than before. I gave the tables a wide berth as I followed him inside, not wanting another annoying sapphire guy to spring to life.

I reached deep inside me for the place where my curse magic—or titan magic, if I believed Cronus, which I'd rather not—lived, grasping it in a tight enough grip that my forearm glowed crimson, a built-in torch that I swept over the shelves I passed.

"Listen to this," Emlyn murmured, jogging down the corridor and into the room, and I jumped when a crackly, distorted voice came from the vague outline of a radio in his hands, the aerial pointing straight up like a rapier. Em twisted the dial until the radio was loud enough for us all to hear, and I edged closer to Verena just in case she needed a hug. Fuck, *I* needed a hug.

"—can now hear from Rone Evans, our New York correspondent. Rone, can you describe what happened when the curtain of darkness fell?"

"It all happened in the space of a few minutes, Sarah. We're still putting the pieces together, but the curtain, as it's being called on social media, blocked out all light sources in various cities across the world. New York was one of the worst hit, and there have been numerous casualties, the majority of which were caused by road collisions where drivers were unable to see the cars around them, or pedestrians unaware they'd walked into the road."

"Shit," Harvey breathed, scrubbing his hand over his jaw. "This is fucked up. So it's everywhere."

"Before they spoke to this woman," Em murmured, "they were talking about London, Paris, Seoul, and Rio."

"Fuck," I breathed, wanting to stay strong and confident for Verena but just ... unable to.

Wynvail struck a match to light one of the candles beside a row of strange, brass globes, but the second the match was lit, darkness swallowed it. I couldn't tell whether the candle was lit. It was like a ghost in Wyn's moonlight. It cast no light.

He blew out the match and threw it aside, his jaw clenched.

Rone Evans continued to talk about the people who'd been caught in accidents because of the curtain, and how stocks were crashing because stockbrokers couldn't see their computers to track the numbers, and even how opportunists had begun to loot shops. Every word she spoke twisted my stomach—and this was happening all across the world.

"Maybe this is a good thing," Wane said quietly. "Maybe we won't have to fight him; all the countries he's hit can send their armies."

"Maybe," Harvey agreed gently.

It seemed unrealistic.

"Well, keep us updated on—" Sarah, the radio presenter began, but a woman's sharp, piercing scream cut her off. "Rone? Can you tell us what's happening? Are you safe? Rone?"

It wasn't Rone who answered; it was a man, and a local judging by his accent. Panic coloured his voice, quickening his words until my hands started to shake.

"The whole road just turned to dust," he screamed. "All the buildings are gone. Some of the people are gone, too. It's the end of the fucking world! I said we shouldn't have made all those memes about the aliens; we pissed 'em off, man."

"I'm sorry," Sarah said to her listeners. "We'll go back to events in New York when we can recover our connection with Rone. It seems her mic was stolen—"

"It's the fucking aliens. The next street just collapsed. Oh fuck, I'm dead. The whole borough's falling. Run for your lives!"

The audio cut off before he could continue, but the damage had been done.

I swallowed, wrapping my arms around my middle, and jumped when a warm hand brushed up and down my back. I leaned into Em with a shaky breath, resting my head on his chest. His heart beat fast but strong—but for how long? How long until Cronus found us, and snuffed us out? He'd just destroyed a whole fucking borough in New York.

"We're—hearing reports of similar events in Moscow," Sarah said, having a hard time keeping her voice calm. Had Rone Evans just been murdered live on radio? Had Cronus turned her to dust like he did to Wyn?

If he wanted us dead, how would we stop him? We had no real shields, no plan, no weapon that could harm him. I only had one of my god-killers, and it hadn't done much good when I had both anyway.

"Oh fuck," Verena choked out, backing up until she bumped into a table. Wyn launched forward and caught her, moving her swiftly out of the way and steadying the jars and potions before they could smash. "That Asta woman was right. He's going to find us, he'll kill us—"

I might have just had those exact same thoughts, but they were sobering coming from a thirteen-year-old.

"He won't," I said gently, my heart pulling tight when Wynvail held Verena's shoulders, looking like he wanted to hug her but wasn't sure how. "I promise you," I swore, having no right to make such promises. "I—I might have an idea how to beat him. I just don't know how the hell to do it. And Wyn has this room—it's full of deadly shit that'll give us an edge."

"What's your idea?" Kai asked, riding a sharp edge of intensity. I held my hand out to him, and he rushed across the narrow room to clasp it. I sent as much calm through the bond as I could when the radio was still listing the damage Cronus had wrought on the world.

"I told you what happened when I died," I murmured, glancing at my family and wishing I could see them properly, not just cast in silver and red by magic. "My soul was protected by shadows—the original darkness. The guy who literally *invented* darkness. Erebus. I get the sense he used to be a super powerful god thousands of years ago. He told me about Cronus, and what his plan is and—why he wanted your shadows so badly, Wane."

Wane straightened, his expression impossible to read in this light and his soul forced calm. Shielded. I hated that his shields were back up.

"Cronus wants your magic because your darkness is inherited from Erebus, and it's true power, in its rawest form. I think that's how you were able to weaken Iapetus," I said, and shut out the memories of that vile bastard. "Your power's different to ours—it's not demon or god or titan or any of that. It's magic from the very start of the universe, and Erebus said it can be used to unmake the world. And remake a very different one."

"Like Cronus did in Olympus," Emlyn murmured, crossing his arms over his chest and hugging his middle.

"He turned it to rubble and remade it in his own twisted image," Wynvail said angrily, sorting through the boxes and shelves beside him, looking for something. "Now it's dark and fucked up and unrecognisable. I'm guessing that's the plan for New York and all those other places."

"When he remakes them," Harvey asked, his hands curling into fists, "do you think that gives him power over those cities? Do you think he can see anyone, anywhere?"

None of us answered. We didn't need to—the answer seemed obvious.

I tightened my grip on Kai's hand; he squeezed back with the same force, terror bouncing from his soul to mine and back to his.

"So if he reduces Edinburgh to rubble, we're screwed," Verena laughed sharply, nothing humorous in the sound at all.

"We're going to be fine," Emlyn said, nothing but calm. "We'll go back to Hell. We'll be safer there—"

"It's my shadow he's using. *My* magic," Wane hissed, the news sinking in—and detonating rage through his soul so vast that I felt it even through his shields. "He stole it from me, and he's using it to do *this?* To demolish whole cities? To wreck homes and livelihoods, to ruin people's lives? To fucking *kill them?*"

Harvey stalked across the room, squeezing past Kai and I, and wrangled his twin into a tight hug. "It's not your fault."

Fuck. My stomach bottomed out.

"Of course it's not," I breathed, my eyes burning. *"None of this* is your fault, Wane. You were captive and tortured."

And if we were playing the blame game, Cronus only managed to harvest one of his shadows when Wane sensed me through the bond, and it made him weak. He would never admit that to me, but I could put two and two together and come up with four. But I was too panicked right now to fully experience self-loathing.

"Why not take over the whole world?" Wane demanded bitterly, hugging Harvey tight. "Why only some cities? He has my shadow—he can remake the whole fucking world. Why not?"

Wynvail riffled through boxes, removing items—and putting them into various satchels. Huh. "Because he can't," he bit out, casting a quick look at Wane before returning to his task. "He only took a small amount of your magic, didn't he?"

"He'd have taken more if you hadn't come for me," Wane muttered.

Harvey yanked on a lock of Wane's chestnut hair, earning a warm look.

"You held out for a hundred years," Wyn said firmly, plundering his shelves next. "Do you have any idea how fucking hard that is? How strong you must be to survive even a year? Fuck, Wane, go a little easier on yourself."

Emlyn nodded emphatically, reaching out to squeeze Wane's shoulder when he disentangled himself from his brother.

"My point is," Wynvail went on, "what if he doesn't have enough shadow magic to take over the whole world? What if he only had enough for these cities?"

"So he chose strategically," Kai muttered. "Picking the most powerful cities, the ones that would screw up human morale the worst."

And it was working. I wasn't even human, and my morale was shot to bits.

"Or this was a test," Wane said, pushing hair from his face, his expression dark and thunderous, "and he'll take over the rest of the world now he knows it works. It's only been an hour since the darkness fell."

"Why isn't this house in ruins?" I murmured, my brows tugging together. "The city's under darkness—the curtain, whatever we're calling it. Why is it not collapsing?"

It wasn't … right? Fuck, if it turned to ash around us, I was going to scream.

"The whole world is under the curtain," Em answered with a calculating look in his eye. "Everywhere's dark, but not everywhere is demolished."

"Because he doesn't have enough shadow magic," Wynvail insisted, giving Wane a firm glance.

I didn't like the sharp bite of bitterness in Wane's soul, but I'd be pretty damn bitter myself after a century of torture and imprisonment. He had every right to the emotion.

"Then he'll come back for more," Wane said, his hands curling into fists, subconsciously mirroring his brother's action.

"That's why I'm packing up the armoury." Wynvail fastened

one of the beige canvas bags and handed it to Wane. "They're as tailored to your skills and magic as I can make them with fifteen minutes' notice. But this shit doesn't come with labels or instructions, so only use it if absolutely necessary. Got it?"

Wane nodded, confused, and peered into the bag.

"Only in emergencies!" Wynvail smacked Wane's hand away, closing the bag and placing it on Wane's shoulder like a mother fussing over her son's first day at school. It melted my panicked heart for a second.

"This is yours, honey," he told me, and handed me a satchel. He scanned my face, searching, worried, and I pasted on a reassuring smile. It was definitely more grimace than smile, but it was the thought that counted. "Look in the front pocket."

I frowned, unbuttoning the utility pocket on the front and reaching inside—

"Mother*fucker!*" I shouted when ice-cold, electric magic deluged my body, burning all the way to my little toes, searing the tip of my tongue, and frazzling my damn eyelashes. I ripped my hand away, confused and touched and close to tears unrelated to the sharp magic. "How?"

A look into the pocket[1] confirmed what I already knew. The bone hair pin sat inside, carved all over with little flowers.

"It must have fallen from Aphrodite's dress when she flew over Olympus. I found it after you ... after," he finished softly.

"So your answer to Cronus destroying half the world is a bag full of goodies?" Harvey asked sceptically, raising an eyebrow when Wyn passed him a bag, too. He peered inside and frowned deeper. "There's a cactus in here."

"Trust me, you'll be glad you have that cactus. Throw it at your enemies," Wynvail said with a little smile. "It's pretty potent when—"

"Verena?" Harvey asked sharply, dumping the bag on the

floor and lurching across the room to grab her hands. "Hey. Look at me."

Her hands were covered in light—not just sparks like usual, but gold pooled in the middle of her palms, dripping through the gaps between her fingers. It splattered the floor, glowing as bright as the sun.

It wasn't the same shade of gold as Harvey's sunlight, the magic he'd used to kill his uncle and destroy the town that shielded the bastard, but it was so similar that I paused, a shudder going down my spine. In an alternate world, her magic would be inherited from Harvey, and she'd be our daughter.

"Verena, look at me," Harvey said gently, holding her hands as magic spilled over.

"I can't control it," she gasped, her eyes distant and lined with tears. "I can't stop it. I'm sorry. I'm sorry."

My heart squeezed tight. She was just a kid. She might have been powerful and fierce and strong as fuck, but she was a kid, and she was scared.

"You don't need to be sorry," Emlyn promised in the soft voice he usually reserved for me. He switched off the radio and set it on the floor, filling the room with static silence. "You've done nothing wrong, Verena."

"We've all lost control of our magic at one point," Harvey murmured. "It's normal. You don't need to be afraid of it—it's your power, no one else's. You're in control of it."

Verena shook her red head, her face so pale. Tears slid from her eyes, carving trails down her cheeks, and my stomach knotted. Some job we were doing of looking after her. We'd made her fucking cry.

"You *are* in control," Harvey insisted calmly. "Your power feels similar to mine, like sunlight." Hers bright and warm, his harsh and unforgiving. "I bet it feels hot, burning in your chest, right?"

She nodded, gasping short breaths, more magic spilling over her hands until tiny pools formed on the floor. Kai motioned for us to move back; Wyn made sure there was no volatile object or potion in its path.

"Sunlight burns; that's just its nature. Don't be scared of it. I'm guessing it's growing with every minute, filling more of you." Verena swallowed and nodded. "But if you close your eyes and reach for your magic, you can push it back into a small ball."

"I can't," she choked out, her voice small.

"You threatened to kick Kai in the balls for stealing your overnight oats this morning," I said, taking a careful step towards them, "and he's a scary fucker. If you can do that, you can do anything."

"Great pep talk," she said weakly, but if she had the energy to sass me, I must have said something right.

"Concentrate," Harvey guided. "Feel where your magic's growing and form it into a ball. You can do this, just take a breath, Verena."

I bit my lip, nervous and helpless and *hating* the feeling. All I could do was watch as Verena wrestled with her magic, tears on her cheeks and her hands shaking. But were the golden drips slowing in frequency? Or was I just seeing what I wanted to see?

"Good," Harvey murmured after a long moment. "Keep pushing."

"I'm not having a baby," she muttered.

Now there was definitely less magic flowing between her fingers. I exhaled a rough sigh of relief. Kai rubbed a hand over his face, squeezing my hand with his other. I leaned back against Em, needing the contact.

"It's stopped," Verena said finally, opening her eyes. There was only a faint pool of gold in her palms. "Thanks," she muttered to Harvey, seeming uncomfortable with the sentiment.

"Any time," Harvey replied with a smile I'd never seen before. It made my heart all squishy and soft. Made me want to cry again.

Everything shifted into a different perspective. We needed to leave Earth, needed to find somewhere safer for Verena, where she wouldn't be stressed twenty-four-seven. Fuck, where *we* wouldn't be stressed.

"You good?" Kai asked her, watching her intently enough that she gave him a strange look.

"I'm fine. What's up with all you weirdos?"

"I told you," Em said fondly. "You're one of us. We worry about our own."

Verena had no reply for that. I knew exactly how she felt. I'd felt the same way when this family welcomed me into them a hundred and ten years ago.

"So," she said, giving us a judgement-heavy look. "Are we going to Hell, or what? Preferably the part of Hell *without* killer ghosts."

A smile began to form, spreading across my cheeks. It fell when Emlyn turned the radio back on and a voice blared through it. Except ... Em was right here. The radio was on the floor with no one near it.

And the voice coming through it was Cronus's.

CHAPTER 19

his is a message from your new ruler.

A gasp caught in the back of my throat, and I moved closer to Kai until we were pressed against each other, hip to hip

"Turn it off!" Wyn hissed, darting for the radio.

Harvey grabbed it first, punching the off switch, but Cronus's painful voice still filled the room.

I am Cronus, first king of the United Earth.

"The united what?" Emlyn demanded, his voice pouring out as a growl and his shoulders broadening, protectiveness surging through his soul.

"It won't turn off," Harvey breathed, the blood draining from his face. "I can't turn it off."

"Listen!" Kai hissed when Cronus spoke again.

I froze, straining my ears, my heart slamming against my ribs.

I have subdued your leaders and liberated you from their disagreements and skirmishes. Instead, every country on Earth will unify under a new leader. I understand this will be a difficult transition for you, so I'll allow you a grace period of three days to adjust.

"But," Wyn muttered, grabbing more assorted magical objects and throwing them into a bag until it bulged.

But I expect your fealty and obedience. Rebellion will not be tolerated.

"There is it," he laughed bitterly, throwing the bag over his shoulder and spearing me with an intense look. "Let's get the hell out of here. There are emergency bags of clothes and supplies in the hallway cupboard."

"You expected this to happen," Kai realised, too freaked out to snarl at Wynvail.

"Not *this*," Wyn sighed, his silver eyes flickering with shadows, memories, "but I knew he'd do something. Here, Verena."

Verena jumped, surprised to be addressed, and accepted a leather satchel a darker shade than ours. Even with my stomach twisting, threatening to evict everything I'd eaten today, my heart turned to mush. He hadn't prepared anything for her, hadn't known she'd be here to provide for, but he *had* provided for her.

And he thought he was a monster?

"What's this?" Verena asked, rifling through the bag as Em and Kai ushered us out of the armoury.

Emlyn made a beeline for the cupboard and found it crammed full of backpacks. I shot Wynvail a soft look he didn't see, my heart bursting out of my chest.

"Explosive," Wyn said sternly. "Put it away."

Verena slid it back into the satchel, smiling.

Rebellion will not be tolerated. Cronus's words rattled around my head, louder each time. I numbly accepted a backpack from Em, hooking it over my shoulder. What were the chances that every world leader left alive said *sure Cronus, we'll roll over and let you invade us?* No chance. No fucking way. But anyone who stood against him would be slaughtered. He killed his own allies—he ate Aphrodite, for fuck's sake. It would be wholesale murder, no one left alive and—

I jumped when cool fingers linked with mine, interrupting my panic with a comforting squeeze.

"We'll be alright," Wane promised, rubbing his calloused thumb over my knuckles. His steady eyes dispelled the sharpest edge of my fear, and I held his gaze like I'd been drowning and he was air.

Wait, was his thumb calloused or was this skin marked with my name, too?

"Everyone ready?" Wynvail asked loudly, drawing my attention away from Wane.

Wyn's back was straight, a serious, capable look on his face that gave me inappropriate butterflies as he scanned our family, making eye contact with each of us. "I have three safe houses in Hell—an apartment in Vollisaw, a house in Jinsevia, and a cottage near the mines in the Kyora mountains. The last house is the one I've shielded the strongest, and it's the biggest so it's probably the best suited to our needs." He looked to me for input. "Is that okay, honey?"

"Anywhere but Jinsevia is fine by me," I replied with a shrug, as much as I could with a heavy backpack. I'd rather not return to the city that housed the war camp I endured for two years. I got out of that place as soon as I could, and I never planned to go within ten miles of the place again. I didn't want Verena anywhere near those bastard soldiers, either.

Judging by the way Wyn's eyes darkened, he knew that part of my history. "Kyora mountains it is. Everyone grab hold of me."

"Aren't the Kyora mountains supposed to be haunted?" Kai asked uneasily, air rippling around his inked arms as his magic manifested.

"Scaredy snake," Harvey coughed.

"They're not haunted," Emlyn interrupted, a growl still

threaded in his voice. "There's a defunct portal there; it's echoes of Earth you can hear."

"Not creepy at all," Kai muttered, but he grabbed Wynvail's arm and the rest of us followed suit. My fingers locked with Wyn's, and I let my eyes close, trusting him to get us out of here. Trusting him, full-stop.

Light pressed through my closed eyelids, and cold bit at my skin through my clothes, raking claws through my wings until a shiver ran through me.

"Don't let go," Wynvail barked, and grunted when I tightened my bruising grip. "Not you, honey. You've already got a stranglehold on my hand."

"So you don't drop me," I bit out, my wings shuddering hard as power raced past my feathers.

"I would never," Wyn swore.

I didn't dare open my eyes to see the maelstrom of magic dragging us across realms. It wasn't legal, per se—we were supposed to use the portals—but there was something to be said for door-to-door travel, and Lucifer couldn't exactly punish us for it, could he?

Fuck, was he dead? Or was he still *alive* in there? Was our king suffering and screaming in Cronus's stomach? My own gut twisted. I wasn't sure I wanted the answer to that question.

"We're here," Wynvail murmured, to a chorus of relieved groans. I opened my eyes, squinting against the prick of lilac daylight. Fuck, I'd missed this light, this realm. Even with everything, I was glad to be home.

"Your magic is bullshit," Verena told Wyn, decidedly green beneath her freckles. "Just so you know."

Wyn tugged on a lock of her hair. "The nausea will only last a few seconds."

As if to prove him wrong, Kai twisted aside and vomited into the grass. I squeezed Wyn's hand and let go, striding across a paved path to Kai's side, and stroking his back while he retched.

"I hate him," he said in a low moan.

"I know," I soothed, pulling wine-red hair out of his face when he heaved again. "I know, my night. He's just awful, how dare he get us to safety."

Kai shot me a betrayed look as he wiped his mouth on his sleeve. "I'm sensing sarcasm."

I leaned in to kiss his forehead. "You sense correctly."

"There's water in the backpacks," Wynvail said, turning to look at the house he'd brought us to. "Just in case someone wanted to get rid of the taste of vomit."

Kai scowled, but I knew it was less because he hated Wynvail and more because he hated being helpless, and sickness fell into that category. Without comment, he fished out the bottle of water and rinsed his mouth, appearing to take great pleasure in spitting it out on the path.[1]

I peered at the house at the end of the brick path. A low, inset pool interrupted the path where a fountain might sit on a fancy French manor, the water reflecting the pale lilac sky like a rectangular mirror. On either side of the pool, a double staircase swept up towards a pale, towering structure with columns, arches, and big bay windows. The mountains were visible in the near distance, but trees framed the house, reminiscent enough of the home that burned down for my eyes to sting.

"Cottage," I said pointedly, staring at the mini-mansion. "How many bedrooms does this *cottage* have?"

"Five," Wyn replied, watching me with eyes gone soft with affection. "Plus three reception rooms, a billiards room, an indoor pool, a library, a weapons room, and a ballroom I thought we could use for training." He paused, and thoughtfully added, "Or balls."

"I'll neuter *your* balls," Kai muttered.

"Don't be sour, Malakai," Wynvail replied with a sharp smile, turning to lead us down the path towards the manor. "My house might be *much* bigger than yours, but I'm sure you make up for it in other ways."

"You're overcompensating for your shrivelled dick," Kai spat, throwing his arm around me and pulling me into his side. "I bet it's tiny. I bet you can't even make Haley come."

I said nothing. Absolutely nothing.

Harvey snorted, watching me with mirth dancing in his mercury eyes and, for once, his face lined with amusement, not deep stress or grief.

"Yours is bigger," I stage-whispered to him.

Besides, we all knew Wane and Em were winning this battle.

"Hey, quick question," Verena input, throwing us all a disgusted look. "Can you maybe keep the dick talk to when I'm *not* within earshot? Thanks."

Harvey grinned. Wyn and Kai both looked equally chastised and apologised, their words overlapping. I fought a smile.

"Smart," I told Verena, ditching Kai and draping my arm across her shoulder. "Stay as far away from anyone with a penis for as long as possible. They're only trouble." I gave Emlyn a sweet smile when he glanced my way, an eyebrow arched. "And if any boy ever gives you hassle, tell me and I'll cut his balls off."

Verena shot me a sideways scowl, her brows low over green eyes. "I can cut their balls off myself."

"I bet I can make them scream louder, though," Kai said, immediately jumping onto the subject. "I know how to cause immense pain."

"Kai," Wane hissed. "Maybe don't scare her...?"

Kai blinked, like it never occurred to him that his words might be anything but normal.

"I could hurt them worse with my sunlight," Harvey input, turning around and walking backwards toward the house to give Verena a bright smile. "If they pissed off our Verena, they'd deserve to suffer obviously."

"Obviously," I agreed with a sage nod.

Verena's eyes had opened from the slits her scowl caused, and a smile spread further across her face with each new word.

Wane noticed it too, and added, "My shadows could make them regret even looking at you. I could make their brains rupture so badly they forgot your name."

"That's the *least* they'd deserve for hurting our Verena," Kai said with a grin, happiness spilling through his soul. "Hey, we could make it a group thing, get the whole family involved."

"Not Em," Harvey and I said at the same time, both our voices hushed.

"Why...?" Verena asked, her attention transferring to Emlyn as he walked with Wyn ahead of us, both probably listening.

"He's a total psychopath," Kai said, pretty ironically given he wrote the book on being a total psychopath. "He'll beat the guy who upsets you into a bloody pulp with his bare hands, until his *species* isn't even recognisable, let alone his face. No one fucks with Em's family and lives."

Verena's eyes were bright, her smile bigger. "You guys are completely insane, aren't you?" she laughed.

"Oh, completely," I agreed, and hooked her closer. "But something tells me you fit in quite nicely."

She peered up at me, wickedness and trauma duelling in her eyes. One day, the trauma would be quieter, and true joy would replace it. The wickedness would probably still be there, though, and I had a feeling the swearing and sarcasm were here to stay.

"You're a bad influence on me," she said, shaking her head.

"You're going to corrupt me until I'm a criminal and bastard like you lot."

We caught up to Em and Wane at the bottom of the sweeping stairs that led to the front door—it was a massive, French door situation because of course it was.

"Nah, Verena. You're the bad influence," I replied with a smirk. "Before I met you, I was soft spoken, never swore, and I was perfectly well behaved."

She snorted and elbowed me. "Don't blame your various mental disorders on me."

Kai laughed this time, loudly enough that he startled a few birds out of the treetops.

"Rude," I told Verena. "Me and my various mental disorders are very offended."

Our smiles lasted as long as it took Wyn to unlock his shields and open the doors, leading us down a high-ceilinged, airy hallway and into a living room where a six-foot tall woman with golden waves of hair and glowing eyes waited by the fireplace.

CHAPTER 20

"Come in," the glow-eyed beckoned with a smile, sweeping a tanned, elegant hand at us.

My breathing cut off in my chest, hairs standing on end along my arms. For a split second I just stared at the woman, stunned still.

Kai reacted instantly, his snakes lashing through the air, and the vibration snapped me out of my stupor. I wrenched on my magic until crimson glowed from my forearm and stomach, and with hasty movements I drew my single volcanic dagger and advanced on the woman.

We all paused when Wynvail jerked forward a step, Verena shielded behind him, and blurted, "Phoebe?"

He knew her? My power flared brighter, jealousy paralysing me until territorialism took its place and gifted my movement back. *Kill first, ask questions later.* I darted around Kai and launched myself at the woman perching far too casually in the beige wingback chair beside the fire. *Our* chair. *Our* fire.

There was a god, titan, *something* in our fucking safe house. A threat.

"Do you know," she asked mildly, "in every possible future, you attempt to kill me right now?" She smiled, even as I drove the point of my dagger at her chest, ruby light pouring down the blade until it glowed vividly.

White magic knocked the tip away before it could pierce her. A sound of frustration rattled my throat, so close to a growl as reverberation shuddered up my wrist. I twisted to glare at Wynvail, fingers clenched white around my knife, and rage filling me so powerfully that Em's chest rumbled with a warning and even Wane scowled, shadows writhing around him to back me up.

"And in every future, he stops you," Phoebe added with a deeper smile. She didn't budge from our chair, completely unruffled with her perfect butter-yellow dress and Stepford-wife hair. Another shudder went down my spine and I retreated three steps.

"She's not a danger to us," Wynvail told the guys and Verena, stalking across the plush rug to me. I spared a single second to look away from the threat, and found a strange gleam in his eyes, almost like Wyn was ... thrilled?

My heart pumped quicker, warning bleating at all my instincts.

"She's also the woman who helped me save your life, Haley. She told me we'd lose you, and we'd need a pearl to bring you back. She's the only reason we still have you, so maybe don't kill her?"

I scowled, unable to let go of my primal violence.

Wynvail smirked and moved into my personal space, his hand sliding across my back. "I can't deny that a part of me is delighted by your show of jealousy. Would you really kill a woman simply because I knew her name?"

"No," I growled.

Yes.

His smirk deepened, a tooth poking free, and he slid his

hand up my back, stroking the edge of my wing until I shuddered. "Liar."

"They're going to kiss," Phoebe whispered. "Should we leave?"

"Ugh, thanks for the head's up," Verena muttered.

Wyn's hand continued until he gripped the back of my neck. "You were going to slit her throat just for looking at me."

I scowled. He had my full attention. "You're mine."

"Yes, I am," he agreed, and dug his fingers into my nape, slamming his mouth into mine until I moaned. He dragged my body against his, his cock pressing insistently against my hip—but I wasn't crazy enough to ride him with a threat in our house. Still, I trusted the rest of our family to handle Phoebe, whoever the fuck Phoebe was, while Wynvail kissed me.

Heat pulsed between my thighs as his rough tongue dominated mine, not letting me take control for even a second. Every stroke and suck short-circuited my brain until my jealousy mellowed to satisfaction. I was still territorial when he drew back, but he was mine, and the whole room was now aware of that.

"You didn't hear a word I said before, did you?" he asked with amusement, like his lips weren't red from our roughened kisses.

"No," I admitted, forcing distance between us and throwing a confident smile at my mates who stood across the room, either watching us or glaring at Phoebe. Wane was absent, but a quick brush along the bond told me he was fine and nearby, probably with Verena. Phoebe was still in the armchair, now staring at the fire instead of us. No one was under any illusions that she was anything other than a threat, no matter what Wyn said. The fearful rage he'd kissed to quietness roared back to life again.

"She saved your life," Wyn repeated, his arm across my

back, less supportive than restraining. If he let go, I'd shoot across the room and rip her throat out. "She warned me what would happen; you're here because of her."

I narrowed my eyes on the flawless, golden woman. "I guess I owe you thanks."

Phoebe glanced up, her eyes trailing over all of us. There was something off about her smile, about the way she held herself, the sweetness of her voice. "I didn't save you from a place of selflessness. I've seen the prophecy on your back."

I stiffened, power blaring from my curse marks, but she went on in an airy, breathless tone, "I know you aim to kill my brother Cronus. The path you're both on now, you and he will be equal when you finally meet. But I can't see who will survive."

"If you just came here to give us creepy prophecies, you can fuck right off," Harvey snapped, stalking across the rug to stand at my side. I settled my hand on his back and sent a rush of comfort through our bond, wincing at the many-fanged panic biting through his soul.

"I came to give you another warning," Phoebe disagreed, frowning at the less than warm reception she was receiving. She rested her joined hands on her knee, her legs crossed under her yellow dress, the very picture of gentility. I didn't buy it. She blinked big, glowing eyes at us and said, "And to tell you how to tip the scales in your favour. I've seen every timeline. Every failure—and each one is because of the prisons."

"The prisons," Harvey murmured, jolting at my side like a bolt of lightning had struck him. "Shit, I forgot about them. Renna and Tali told us about them while we were in Olympus —Cronus is keeping gods and their kids in them. There are four of them."

"Five," Phoebe corrected, fluttering a hand. "One is so

secret no one else knows of it—it's where his most powerful victims are kept. As long as the prisons are full, you will lose."

"I'm not fighting him," I snarled, my stomach twisting up into a pretzel. "I'm done. I'm not going anywhere near Cronus, so it doesn't matter how many people he—eats. It won't affect us."

Phoebe gave me a pitying look that got my hackles up. Emlyn growled in sympathy, but the prophet, goddess, *whatever* was unaffected by his warning.

"Either you go to him, or he will come to you; there's no escaping a prophecy." Her smile turned sad, her eyes downcast, almost genuine. "I was the one who prophesied the words inked on your back, do you know? He pulled out my fingernails and branded me on the wounds until I could do nothing but scream for mercy. I'd determined to never give him what he wanted, but he always wins." When she lifted her head and smiled wider, I saw the true predator in her and I inhaled sharply, shuddery all over. "The prophecy didn't give him what he wanted though. Futures are like that. He wanted proof of his invincibility, but instead found his demise."

I reached for my mates' souls, making sure we were all safe, and couldn't escape the horror of how casually Phoebe spoke about someone ripping out her fingernails and *branding* the nail beds.

"I've had my fingernails ripped out so many times I've lost count," Wane's soft, raspy voice made me jump as he appeared in the doorway, with Verena pale-faced but glaring at his side. "That doesn't mean we're going to put Haley in danger. You heard what she said—we're not fighting Cronus. We're *done.*"

"You can't outrun fate," Phoebe whispered, the temperature of the sitting room dropping dramatically. I shivered violently, the shudders finally ripping free when an unnatural golden haze spilled across the room, staining neutral furniture, warm brown walls, and every one of my family in butter-yellow light.

I shot Verena and Wane a hard look and they hurried across the room to us, showing a unified front of weapons and magic.

She laughed, the sound not remotely human, and added, "But you're welcome to try. You will die. All of you—and there will be no coming back this time."

Goosebumps rose all down my body, power hanging in the air like a veil, blurring everything, as Phoebe rose from her seat by the fire. My gut clenched. I needed to run but—my feet wouldn't move. Oh god, I was trapped.

She cast a slow stare over all of us, no longer smiling. "I helped you once, Wynvail, and you ignored me. You almost lost everything."

Wyn clenched his jaw, his eyes straying to me.

"Don't make that mistake twice. There is no escaping Cronus; there is only defeating him. The prisons are his buffet. Empty them."

Her glowing gaze shifted to me, and tingles of screaming warning covered my body, her power triggering my flight instincts like crazy. I waited for pain, waited for her to seize control of my body, but neither happened. I knew she could crush the life out of me with zero effort. Why didn't she?

Who *was* she? I really should have done more research into mythology when I had downtime.

"Your friend is in the worst prison. He'll devour her soon."

"Renna," I gasped, resuming the ability to speak when her stare moved to Emlyn. Cold premonition sluiced down my spine, or maybe that was a cold sweat.

Threatening or creepy or not, I didn't think Phoebe was lying. It made sense. There was no doubt this goddess had her own agenda, but how did Renna play into it? How did we?

"Fuck," Kai breathed, trembling with restraint or rage beside me.

When Phoebe's attention drifted to Verena, Harvey and I moved swiftly, hiding her behind us while everyone else surrounded her in a protective swarm.

"Don't even *look* at her," Emlyn growled at Phoebe, his whole body swelled and bulging with muscle.

I blinked and shadows erupted around us, a protective wall slamming down between us and the threat.

"This is overkill," Verena muttered behind me.

"You were fathered by Apollo," Phoebe said to her, some of the otherworldliness leaving her, the gold haze fading from the air. "Apollo is my grandson. You have the same eyes."

I bared my teeth, pointing my dagger at her.

"She's ours," Wane said in a low voice full of shadows and menace before I could speak that exact claim.

Phoebe smiled, back to her dreamy, sweet, *wouldn't hurt a fly* persona.

My dagger burned in my hand; I literally itched to throw it at her face. I owed her my life, so she would walk out of here with hers intact. The next time we met? All bets were off.

"Yes," Phoebe agreed, drifting back a step, possibly because she couldn't breach Wane's shadows. "She is yours. Others who are yours are inside Cronus. Empty the prisons, and they will be saved, and you all might survive."

"And if we don't?" Wynvail challenged, catching my elbow to keep me close, probably sensing I was one false move away from unleashing all hell.

"Fate will find you and kill you." Phoebe looked over all of us, her eyes gleaming gold. "You may be archdemons, and descendants of gods and titans with Fury in your heart, but as long as Cronus has that power at his disposal, you will not survive."

I wanted to turn to look at Em, to see if he still meant what he said in the training room about wanting Cronus dead. I promised Kai and Harvey we were finished with battles and fate, but when I blinked, I saw Renna's face, and the double beat of my heart echoed two words over and over.

Kill him. Kill him.

CHAPTER 21

I expected an argument of epic proportions. Or maybe we'd all be civilised demon beings for once and we'd have a debate, a real *conversation* instead of shouting, snarling, and storming off in a sulky huff. I didn't expect Em to say we needed to get Renna out of the prison ASAP, and then we need the bastard dead even ASAP-er, and for everyone *to agree.* I didn't know what alternate world we were living in, but even Harvey heaved a sigh and submitted. Kai glared daggers at us but muttered, "Fine," which was exceptionally calm for him.

I wasn't the only one who trusted Wynvail, apparently. If he believed Phoebe was telling the truth, the rest of us did. And deep down we all wanted to make Cronus bleed and scream and suffer, and we had a way to make that happen. We didn't have to fight him; we just had to empty the prisons.

Renna would do it for us. She came to fight for me in Olympus. Em was right; it was killing me to leave her there.

We were all gathered in the second living room now, deeper in *the cottage*[1] where it was warmer and felt more protected. Bonus: there was no creepy, threatening prophetess waiting for us in this room. The décor here was as neutral as the rest of the house, but an exposed brick wall on the back was interrupted by a small window looking out on the forest instead of vulnerable double glass doors. I might have been delusional, but there was just something comforting about having walls made of actual brick. Plus, the room was full of fluffy rugs, throws, and cushions, and if I leaned just slightly, I could see the sheen of shadows and moonlight shielding the house.

Kai sat on top of me on the beige sofa, like a Great Dane convinced they were a lap dog, and Wane was equally entrenched in my personal space, his side flush to mine and shadows wrapped around my arm from wrist to shoulder. I tried to send an equal amount of comfort to all my mates, scared I'd neglect someone when they needed me, but cutting myself into five equal parts wasn't the easiest thing to do. We were all freaked the fuck out by Cronus taking over Earth, and even more unsettled by the fact we were walking voluntarily into one of his prisons.

Or buffets as Phoebe called them. Phoebe *the titan,* as it turned out. Mother of Leto and Asteria, and grandmother of Apollo and Artemis. Even I'd heard of those gods, and it only made it more remarkable that we'd escaped our encounter with Phoebe unscathed.

I wasn't sure how to feel about a titan being the reason I was alive, or the creator of the prophecy I was marked with. If I thought about it too hard, my head would spin. I was a normal, run-of-the-mill demon, and yet my life was unfolding like I was living in a myth itself.

Harvey blew out a sigh, an insistent discomfort itching though his soul as he pushed out of the armchair he'd sat in and dropped to the floor in front of me. The sensation faded into relief when I ran my fingers through his shaggy brown hair, so I wrapped comfort and reassurance around his soul and hoped it didn't feel like a lie.

I'd meant it when I promised to never join a war again. We couldn't sit back and let Renna be murdered, tortured, or eaten—or all three. But voluntarily walking back into a place owned and controlled by Cronus felt a lot like walking back into the Damned House, and guilt bit into my stomach.

We were ringing the damn dinner bell; Cronus would come running and devour us. Devour me. Again.

I was relieved when Em strode into the living room, making my lips twitch into a smile when he sank into the chair Harvey just vacated and kicked off his shoes.

"You have a cute little hole in your sock," I pointed out.

He laughed tiredly. "If you find it cute, Hales, I'll leave it there. Not that I have much time for darning socks lately."

My chest warmed when he met and held my gaze, and I felt stronger for having him in sight, for having his eyes on me.

"So," I said, licking my dry lips. "We're racing back into danger."

"Armed to the teeth this time," Harvey pointed out, leaning his head into my hand when I forgot to keep stroking his hair. I resumed, and he released a long sigh. "Wynvail's bags of danger should make a difference. It's not like Cronus is actually going to be at the prison. He's busy running around the world, destroying cities and rebuilding them."

"Bags of danger," Wyn repeated with a low laugh, slumping into the room looking even more tired than Em. I needed more arms so I could hug all of them. It really wasn't fair that he had to cross the room and drop into the other chair, barely suppressing a groan. We'd been happy for *a day*, and now all the aches and weariness had returned. "Talking about my eye bags, are you?"

Harvey snorted. "Yeah, those things are massive. Have you

ever thought about using makeup? You look like you lost a boxing match."

Wyn gave him the middle finger, but he was unable to hide his smile.

Surliness came from Kai's soul. He glowered, resting his head on my shoulder.

"Don't be jealous," I teased him, kissing the sharp edge of his cheekbone. "I'm sure Harvey still loves you."

"Shut up," Kai muttered.

"If you want me to bring up your dark circles, too," Harvey drawled, turning to throw a smirk at Kai, "I'm more than happy to. I just didn't want to kick a man while he was down."

Kai narrowed his eyes. "Meaning..."

"That dead fox you're wearing as hair these days," Harvey replied innocently. "You've got enough trouble grooming that thing without—motherfucker!" he shouted, the air vibrating with one of Kai's snakes.

"I'll poison you," Kai hissed, the light returning to his eyes. "Don't tempt me."

I relaxed into the sofa with a smile, stroking a finger over the shadow wrapped around my arm until Wane slumped against me with a slow breath. Balance was restored. And honestly, Harvey was a sarcastic little shit that loved to wind people up; Kai should know by now he had enough insults for both him and Wynvail.

"What is it?" Wane asked—Wynvail? I was expecting Em, but Emlyn's head was tipped against the chair back, and he was close to nodding off. My heart went all melty and gooey even if we really needed him to help us plan the prison break.

"Verena needs therapy," Wyn replied, running a hand over his brown hair. It was a lot more unkempt lately, like we were *all* more unkempt. It was hard to take care of yourself when you were trapped in a cycle of grief, depression, and fighting for your life. I called it a win when I remembered to wash my pits and under-boob areas. "I left her in the kitchen with a steak and a meat tenderiser," he added. "I couldn't think of anything else."

Kai exhaled a soft laugh. "She's going to murder that steak."

"I'll still eat it," Harvey reassured him.

"You'll eat anything," Wane remarked, nudging his brother with his foot.

"We probably all need therapy," I murmured, meeting Wyn's serious gaze. "Especially lately. But—you're right. When we've got Renna out of the prison, we'll find someone to help Verena. Lili might know someone."

Wane slid the spiral-hilt knife I gave him out of its sheath, turning it over and over in his hands. "I don't want to talk to anyone."

"Ditto," Kai agreed instantly, his eyes glowing. "My shit's mine. No one needs to know it."

"Not even me?" I asked, stroking the spiky defensiveness on the other end of our bond until the sharp edges smoothed.

"Of course I'll talk to you, my rose," he promised, but I got the sense it was only because he couldn't say no to me and not because he wanted to talk.

I pressed a kiss to his cheek, my lips lingering. "But before therapy and all that sensible shit—how are we going to break into a prison that belongs to Cronus? *Without* catching his attention. I don't want to see that monster again. Ever."

Wane's shadows tightened on my arm. The air trembled with Kai's power. I saw the memories of losing me in each of their eyes; Em was wide awake now, any peace sleep had promised him wiped away.

"We don't—have to do this," Kai said hesitantly, his eyes averted from me even as he remained on my lap. "I know Renna helped us, and she's a friend, but—is it worth the risk?

To put ourselves back on Cronus's radar? For him to have undeniable proof Haley is still alive?"

"Yes," I answered in a hiss, my voice sharper than it had been since Phoebe left. Their panic banged around my chest like a pinball—or a wrecking ball—but I forged on, "Renna came for us in Aphrodite's prison. She helped get us out. We're returning the favour, and it's not up for debate."

"So this relationship is a dictatorship," Kai muttered, scowling at all the places our bodies aligned.

I sucked on a tooth, my blood roaring, but ... he was right.

So I sighed and said, "Alright, then we'll vote. Raise your hand if you think we should rescue Renna."

Em, Harvey, and I raised our hands.

Wane, Kai, and Wyn didn't.

Shit, it was equal.

"I vote we go," Verena said, making us all jump when she appeared in the doorway, a bronze orb in her hand glowing with bright golden sunbeams.

"You're not coming, so you don't get a vote," Kai argued, instantly protective. I had a weird flash forward to him saying, *you're not going out in that skirt* in our future and for a moment I smiled.

"Alright," Verena agreed placidly. I didn't trust it for a second. "Then who's staying behind to babysit me?"

She grinned when we looked at each other, at a loss for an answer. We couldn't leave her here alone. But bringing her with us was out of the question, too.

"Cool, then I'm coming," she chirped, striding over to the sofa and plopping onto the arm beside me. "Also, I made this. I did the thing you told me to do when I lost control, Harvey. It worked. Kinda. I was looking through my bag at all the fun, dangerous shit you gave me, Wynvail, and I still had this sphere thing in my hand. I got control of my power—"

"That's amazing, Verena," Harvey breathed, getting to his feet. "Seriously."

"But now I have a glowing sphere." She held it up, its light casting across the coffee table and sofa. "Cool, huh?"

"What does it do?" I demanded, fixing a stare on Wyn as he stood and approached slowly. Too slowly, like you'd approach a bomb ticking down.

The magic's light caught his eyes and turned them to pure, metallic gold. "According to the woman I bought it from, it can create a separate world about as big as a house that stands apart from every other realm in the universe."

"So it'd be useful in a fight," Verena said with a sharp grin I didn't like at all.[2] "And I'm coming with you. *Unless* you'd like to leave me all alone, in a huge scary house in the middle of Hell, where *anything* could happen to me."

"Oh, she's good," Wane said with a soft laugh, leaning against me.

Verena knew she'd won. Victory glittered in her eyes. "Good. So, we're saving Renna and breaking into a prison. Maybe not in that order. What's the plan?"

"Put the orb away and we'll talk," Wynvail said, not taking his eyes off it.

Verena shrugged and got up to put it back in her bag.

"Phoebe showed me the location of all the prisons," Wyn said when she returned. His mouth twisted, and a shimmer of unease went through his soul. "I wasn't aware she could speak directly into my head, but I don't know why I'm surprised. The prison is built into Mount Ida."

I didn't understand the heavy, sympathetic look he gave me. "What?"

"It's a significant location," he said gently. Why was he talking like that? I scowled.

Emlyn sent me a rush of strength and love. Why did I need

strength and love? "Mount Ida was where Zeus was born, and where he spent most of his childhood."

So...?

"It's where Rhea lived for many years. There are still monuments and temples to her there."

Oh. My stomach knotted. I swallowed and nodded. "Got it."

It was special to my great-grandmother. Who I killed the same day I met her.

I wasn't fooling anyone with my *everything's fine* mask; my mates pressed closer in all of my bonds, offering comfort. I knew, deep down, I didn't kill her. But it was my hand holding the knife, and my blade that killed her. It felt a lot like it was my fault.

"I'm missing something," Verena said, frowning between us.

I detangled myself from Wane and pushed Kai off my lap, getting to my feet, needing to move. "What else did Phoebe tell you, Wyn? I don't suppose she gave you a how-to of breaking into a megalomaniac's prison?"

"No," he replied softly. "But she did tell me we have the best shot at being successful if we breach the prison at exactly 09:02 tomorrow morning."

I spun on the rug, staring at my mate in horror. "Not tonight? We have to wait until tomorrow?"

He nodded.

"I can't wait until tomorrow." I had all this energy. I needed to get going, get fighting, I needed—therapy. Shit, I really did. These were not very smart coping mechanisms.

"We'll take the night to come up with a plan and make sure it's fool-proof," Em assured me, catching me before I could pace and pulling me into his side. "We'll make sure nothing goes wrong."

As opposed to running hastily into a prison because I

couldn't sit still. Okay, fair enough, mistakes would have been made.

"And it gives us time to track down Asta," Verena pointed out. "She'll probably murder everyone to get to her wife, and you lot won't have to get your knives dirty."

That sounded lovely. Unrealistic but lovely.

"So we're going back to Greece," Harvey mused, running a hand through his hair.

"Crete," Wyn corrected. "Mount Ida's in modern-day Crete."

Harvey blinked. "Which is in Greece."

I tuned them out, trying out a smile as I glanced at Wane. "Do you want to spar? I could use a way to get rid of all this energy."

And it seemed to help Wane that morning his memories kept him from sleep. Since we had *hours* until we could take any kind of action ... I needed something to do. Now we'd decided to act, waiting was driving me insane.

"As long as you don't cheat," he replied with an easy smile.

I forgot how to breathe. Godsdamn, he was beautiful. And mine. How the fuck was he mine? It made zero sense, but I wasn't about to complain that an Adonis like Wane wanted someone as surly, spiky, and foulmouthed as me. I wasn't insecure, not after ten years with him, but still very baffled.

"I never cheat," I assured him, affronted. "I've never once cheated in my life."

Kai snorted loudly. Rude.

"I'll make something to eat," Em offered, heading for the door after he'd swept his gaze over all of us twice, checking we were okay. "I want to bake. We need some more bread."

"There's a loaf already in the bread bin," Wynvail said helpfully, but Em shook his head and left the room.

"It's his stress thing," I told Wyn. "Baking. It helps."

"Wow." Verena blinked, her freckled face slack with

surprise. "A healthy coping mechanism? I'm shocked. What are your stress things? Murder and disembowelment."

I exchanged a swift glance with Kai and Harvey.

"No," Harvey protested.

"Embroidery," Kai said so seriously I might have fallen for it.

"Oh, speaking of," I said, hooking my arm with Kai's when he got to his feet, seeking more touch. "I want you to needle-point me a pillow. With a cute, widdle bunny wabbit on it. I want it to have a baby pink bow."

Kai snorted and shoved me into Wane who caught me easily, his hands feathering down my wings. I immediately thought of ways to cheat while sparring so I could feel his hands on more places.

Verena smirked and shook her red head. "Fucking weirdos."

"Aww," Harvey breathed, his mercury eyes big and round. "Her first term of endearment for us." He pretended to wipe a tear and we laughed, all pretending to be completely, ordinarily fine. Denial? Here? No, sir.[3]

Verena rolled her eyes hard. "I'm going to explore the house. Enjoy your needle—whatever the fuck it is."

"I will," Kai assured her fiercely. He'd carry that lie to his death.

When I headed for the door, my arm linked with Wane's, Kai halted me with my name. His amusement had faded, a furrow between his dark red brows.

"Later, I want to take a look at your back. I—" He sighed heavily. "I've never read the full prophecy. I didn't want to know any of it. But I think we're going to need it now. If Phoebe's right, that fate's coming for us no matter what we do. We should at least find out what we're up against."

I really wished I didn't agree with him, but I couldn't find a reason to disagree. So I nodded and promised to find him later.

But I really didn't want to know what great and terrible fate awaited me. Hadn't my life already been great and terrible enough?

CHAPTER 22

KAI

"You look like you're walking to the gallows," I remarked, my eyes on Haley as she approached the table in the cluttered library room where I'd been pouring over mythology books for the last two hours. Harvey had helped me at first, but something in one of the books made him slam it shut and storm out of the room, muttering about having better shit to do. The old myths were full of assault and rape; it didn't take a genius to see he was remembering what had happened to him. But he ran off before I could bring him out of it, and this was too important to leave.

Cronus had been around for hundreds of years—millennia even—and these books might read like fairy tales and fiction, but they were real. They were full of his strengths, weaknesses, and motives. He might have been powerful enough to rule the world, but he could be outsmarted.[1]

I marked my page and closed the book I was reading, fixing my full attention on Haley. My stomach had been knotted since I said I wanted to read the prophecy on her back, but for a second all I felt was boiling, insistent lust as I watched my mate approach. A fine sheen of sweat covered her skin, her inked arms bared by a sleeveless black shirt, the fine muscle in her biceps making my cock jump to life in my pants. The messy ponytail and the loose, confident way she walked certainly didn't hurt. I wanted her to climb onto my lap and ride me to ruination. Wanted her to own me, *wreck* me. Part of me was still feral, a very big part of me still broken; I'd just pulled the jagged pieces back together and taped them in place. I was still in the shower in Edinburgh, empty and terrified to lose her again.

But the nervousness in Haley's expression cleared my head —even if it didn't quite deter my dick—and when she bit her lip, the gravity settled back onto my shoulders.

"Aren't I walking to the gallows?" she laughed tightly, perching her fine ass on the edge of the table. I was distracted for a moment by tracing my palms up her thighs, but I batted the need back when she spoke. "This prophecy probably says how I'm going to die—preferably in a blaze of blood and glory, but probably doing something dumb like trying to stab a titan in his big toe."

My lips twitched into a smile, and I met her gaze, holding eye contact. "It's going to be alright."

Her little laugh disagreed with me; she looked away. "Nice place, this. Very cosy. I like the amber lighting—and that heavy oak really warms up the place."

"Haley," I murmured, squeezing her hips.

"Em's always wanted a library. It's a step up from the three cluttered bookshelves we had in our last home." Not the safe house in Edinburgh—the house where we'd lived for years, where we'd felt safe. Until Wynvail burned it down. Traitorous, villainous, heinous— "Why are you suddenly murderous, Malakai?"

I blinked innocently. "Just thinking about Cronus."

She bit her lip again; I rolled it free with my thumb, stroking the dent she'd made.

"I was glad, you know?" she blurted, meeting my eyes with something close to panic. I slid my fingers into her pink hair and cradled the back of her head, knowing it comforted her. "When I couldn't read it, when I found out it was written in the old language. Then, I never had to find out what the prophecy said."

"Except you have a mate who can read it," I murmured, stroking her scalp with the pad of my thumb. "Whatever it says, it changes nothing. You're not a slave to fate, my rose. This only foretells what you *choose* to do. That's how destinies work."

She scoffed. "Phoebe made it sound like we can't fight it. Like fate's going to grab my body and pilot me like a puppet."

"That's *not* going to happen," I said firmly, though I truly had no idea how fate worked. Fate was the reason Haley was my mate, and I wouldn't change this bond for anything in any world, but even if we'd hated each other, would Fate have pushed us together and given us no choice? I decided I didn't care. She was mine, and overthinking it would just make my head explode. I had enough worries without adding another. "I mean it, Haley, this changes nothing. Whatever it says, you're still a badass woman with a crazy streak, a massive heart, and a killer ass."

"Thanks," she drawled, but she was smiling.

"And you have your mates beside you," I added. "Always. It's not your prophecy, my rose; it's ours."

Her pale throat bobbed. "Fine. Let's get it over with."

She hopped off the table and pulled her sweaty shirt over her head, peeling off her bra next.

"I could bend you over this table and fuck you until you scream," I pointed out.

"Or you could read the prophecy of my guaranteed-to-be-grizzly death."

Right. A bucket of metaphorical ice dumped over me. "Turn around, my rose. And don't worry." I rose from my seat and moved closer, dropping a long kiss on your shoulder. "I'm right here. I've got you."

She nodded, a tremor going through the tether between us. I kissed her other shoulder for good measure and stepped back, steeling myself before I began to read. I'd only glimpsed a single line before—*what is made can be unmade*—and immediately looked away. If this did speak of her death, I wouldn't be able to handle it. I couldn't lose her again. She was my entire goddamn world, and I didn't want anything to do with a universe without my—

"Kai," she said urgently. "Tell me."

I shook my head to knock some sense into my brain and began to read the dark words inked lovingly down her spine. My stomach twisted into a tight knot the more I read.

"WHAT IS DEAD CAN LIVE ANEW
   When bonds are shattered, love runs true
   Kin is found and lost once more
   A titan's death brings final war
   What is made can be unmade
   At Olympus, steep price is paid
   Sacrifices, thefts, and gifts bestowed
   When archdemon's final seeds are sowed
   King's final stand, titan's last breath

A hellborn angel will deliver death
Gods, mortals, and titans all
Will bring the end at shadow fall."

I BLINKED, READING IT AGAIN, AND AGAIN.

"Wait, that's it?" Haley demanded. "His final breath? How is that supposed to help me? I thought it would say how to kill him, or how I'd die or—something more than this crappy poem an angsty teenager could have written."

"Verena could have done a better job," I agreed, not sure what my emotions were doing. "Phoebe's a shit poet, that's for sure."

I traced the words inked on Haley's back, licking my dry lips. "The first two lines are self-explanatory—our murder, rebirth, and finding our bonds again. The next ... a titan's death. Rhea?"

Haley nodded, pink hair falling across her back; I moved it aside to read the next two lines. "What is made can be unmade; at Olympus, steep price is paid. That's Wynvail and —you."

Steep price. Yeah, there was no steeper fucking price than this war talking my mate from me. I still hadn't come back from it. I brushed a kiss to the place a wing met her shoulder, inhaling a slow breath of her scent. It was the only thing that helped me settle sometimes—having her scent in my lungs. I knew that was the Feral in me, knew I was still every bit as animalistic as I was at Alphaven. Deep down under all the pieces Haley had repaired, my core was unchanged.

"I'm right here, Kai," Haley soothed me, reaching around her sides for my hands. "Here, feel."

A surprised laugh burst out of me when she pressed my hands to her boobs. I helped myself to a squeeze, running my thumbs across her nipples.

"Definitely here," I agreed, strangely comforted by the gesture. A breath punched out of me, and I read the next lines of the prophecy. "Sacrifices, thefts, and gifts bestowed when archdemon's final seeds are sowed. Any ideas, my rose?"

"Maybe my sacrifice? When I died? Maybe Wyn's? Thefts, though… Have we stolen anything lately?"

"Not that I remember. Maybe we stole you from death with the resurrection pearl."

She made a thoughtful hmm. "What about the seeds sown bit?"

I nipped the sensitive arch of her wing. "We've definitely sown a few seeds in your pussy."

She elbowed me. "Be serious, Malakai."

I laughed, kissing the same spot until she shuddered, her nipples pebbling under my hands, her skin hot and soft and so fucking tempting. "Archdemon's final seeds. That's probably us. Maybe we're going to plant a garden. Or maybe it's talking about a seed of magic."

"Yeah, I have no idea what that means either. Maybe Em will know."

"Maybe Harvey will surprise us and say something insightful for once."

She elbowed me again. "You do realise he's not around to hear you antagonising him?"

"I'm hoping he'll sense the disturbance in the air."

Haley snorted. "What's the next line?"

"King's final stand, titan's last breath; a hellborn angel will deliver death. Other than telling us you'll kill him, which we already knew, what does it say?"

"It's all tied into the archdemon seeds and sacrifices part," Haley groaned. "Of course it hinges on the line we're blanking on. *Of course* it does."

"Maybe fate will help you figure out the meaning at the exact right time," I suggested. She scoffed, but I was serious.

Clearly whichever deity decided our fate was paying attention; Phoebe saw all this happen and wrote the prophecy, but some higher power was watching, guiding us.

"And the next line?" she asked.

"The last one," I murmured. "Gods, mortals, and titans all will bring the end at shadow fall."

"Is shadow fall a place?" she mused, leaning into me and no doubt feeling my hardness pressing against her ass. "Or a time? An event?"

"I can make a shadow fall," I said. "I'll just stick my foot out and trip Wane the next time I see him."

"Hilarious," Haley drawled, but her soul rushed around mine, her fear bright and loud but comfort was there too, like I made a difference, like I gave her the same strength she gave me. She was a fucking gift; being able to comfort her was a gift. I'd never take it for granted again.

"There's no mention of another death," I pointed out, letting my lips linger on her shoulders, tasting her skin. "Only the one that took you and Wynvail already."

"Yeah, because the prophecy is about Cronus's dying. He'll probably take us with him, but Phoebe didn't bother writing that because we're an addendum to the more important death."

That hadn't occurred to me. My chest tightened at the thought, and I dropped my hands from her boobs so I could wind my arms around her.

"Shit, that was thoughtless," she muttered, settling her hands over my arms and squeezing. "I'm sorry."

"It's fine," I bit out, visions and memories flashing behind my eyes. Being frozen in place, helpless, while she fought Cronus alone. The scent of blood in the air—my mate's blood—when he ripped the knife out. The knife I gifted her. The emptiness in her eyes, the limp fall of her arms, the slackness of her face. The cold, icy numb that froze our bond.

"Kai," she murmured, turning in my arms and catching my face in a rough grip, digging in her fingernails until the prick of pain drew me out of it. "Look at me; I'm right here. And you're right, the prophecy doesn't say anything about us dying, so that must be positive."

But she'd put the idea in my head now and it would not be evicted.

She kissed me suddenly, desperately, and a groan caught the back of my throat. My hands flexed on her hips as her tongue parted my lips, taking control of me in a way that made my gut clench and my balls ache.

"Haley," I breathed, husky and raw.

"Back with me?" she asked, panting, her lips red and wet, tempting me back for another taste.

"I'm with you," I swore, and kissed her again, surrendering when she dominated the kiss, far too thrilled with the way she controlled me to fight back. Her sweet taste invaded my senses, wrapped around my tongue until I couldn't remember any other taste, and a deep, throaty groan escaped me when she threw a leg around my waist and ground against me. Heat boiled up in my cock, need a fucking furnace in my blood, pounding with unrelenting demand.

I knew it was a fear response, but I didn't give a shit. I needed to be inside her *now*.

"Question," she gasped when we parted, her breathing hard in a way that felt like an accomplishment. "This was written in the old language."

"That's not a question," I pointed out, fastening my lips to her throat and kissing down to her collarbone.

"Whose old language is it?"

I paused, drawing back. Blinking. I … didn't know.

"It looks nothing like any other demon language," she said, reading my confusion through the bond. "So who made it? Where did it come from?"

"I don't know. I don't think my mum ever knew, or my grandfather who taught her to read and write it. It's just ... something we all knew. All the demons in our community can read it. We inherited traditions and language and stories, and it was drummed into us to keep them alive, to never let them be forgotten."

"What stories?" Haley's brow was knotted when I unfolded to my full height, surprise dulling my desire.

I shook my head, not because I didn't know but because— this felt important, like we were on the edge of something, and I couldn't believe it. Her prophecy being inked in the language of my people couldn't be a coincidence, but I didn't know how all the puzzle pieces fit together.

"Most were stories of the first beings, from the very beginning of the universe." I swallowed at the full weight of Haley's attention, but very quickly summarised, "Chaos came to be, the first being in the universe, and from Chaos came the Earth, and the Abyss, and Love, in that order. After them came Darkness and Night. From the first beings came all of creation.

"The stories are ... our origins. They're not really gods, and I know what you're thinking but they're not titans either. They're primordial, primitive, from the earliest days of Hell, their stories passed down through generations."

Haley was smiling. It was disturbing, that smile, given the gravity of her prophecy. "The stories are real, Kai."

I shook my head. "They're only stories, Haley. They're as real as any fairytale—"

"Except I've met one of those first beings."

I jolted, staring at her. It took a moment for those words to fully compute. "You ... that's *impossible*. They created the universe, my rose. They made the world—every speck of life, the sun and moon, the ground we stand on, this damn house

—they made all of this and there's no way you could have met one."

She rolled onto her toes to kiss me. "The Darkness at the beginning of the world. I know he's just the Darkness in your people's stories, but he's also called Erebus, and he's a right grumpy bastard. Likes to list his titles *constantly* and he's a big fan of giving self-righteous lectures."

My head spun, the two very separate stories connecting—the Darkness at the beginning of creation and Erebus, who saved my mate and cared for her until she was able to return to us. She—

"You met *a first being?*" I demanded, my voice shrill. "What the fuck, Haley?"

"If you know stories about Erebus, maybe you know stories about Cronus too, right? What do you know about the god of time?"

I swallowed, resistant. I didn't want to tarnish the stories my mum told me by connecting them to the cunt who killed my mate.

"Kai," Haley murmured, stroking fingers through my hair and sending a ripple of sensation down my spine.

"He was the ruler of all beings, after he slew the Sky." I groaned and felt like a fucking idiot. "Cronus killed his father Uranus, the god of the Sky. Fuck!" How was this so damn obvious when I said it out loud?

"It's okay," Haley soothed, nothing but calm and love in her storm-grey eyes. "You weren't looking for titans in your stories; of course you wouldn't realise."

I ran through all the stories in my head, my mother's voice so close that my throat closed up, the words choked. "Time was a jealous being, always coveting what others had—land, power, magic, titles, women. He was never satisfied, always yearning for more. And he was brave, strong—able to do what others didn't dare, like killing his father."

My stomach squirmed at badmouthing one of the first beings I'd been taught to respect all my life.

"But he was a good ruler, nothing like the psychopath he is now. I think—either our stories are wrong, and it was never a golden age of peace and prosperity when he ruled, or being imprisoned in Tartarus fucked with him."

"He's jealous and greedy," Haley said, her fingers sifting through my hair. "We can use that. Make him want something we have, spring a trap."

"He's not just the god of time, Haley, he *is* time. Do you have any idea how much he can fuck with us?"

"According to the ink on my back, we can fuck with him right back. We just need to steal something and gift some seeds."

Her words didn't draw me from my panic so much as the rush of power I felt through her did.

I paused, holding her tighter. "Cronus helped Locke kill us the first time because he wanted to concentrate your power," I said.

"Yup. Fattening me for the slaughter," she said bitterly.

"You just—died again," I said, my heart beating harder.

"I don't feel any different," she replied, reluctant to kill that hope. "But hey, maybe I can grow as massive as Cronus and go all shadow-giant, too."

I nodded absently, stories echoing around and around my head. They were all I could think of: every bedtime tale and fireside story merging into something far more real than simple folklore. They were real—the first beings. And my mate was fated to kill one of them.

I jumped when Haley's hands settled on my shoulders, manhandling me back into the chair I'd been sitting in before she arrived. My ass met the seat hard, and I frowned at her, unsure where the dark gleam in her eye had come from.

"You always tell me I think too hard," she murmured,

making my heart stop by dropping to her knees in front of me. "And I need to shut off my mind for a while."

"I do," I agreed, my voice rougher, deeper. She made a pretty picture, her chest bare and her beautiful rosy tits on display for me, her tattoos decorating her arms and stomach, painting her like an artwork as she knelt before me.

But I didn't have time to shut off my mind—we had until tomorrow morning to come up with an ironclad plan to get into a titan's prison and out again safely, *without* letting him know we were there. Not that I held much faith in the latter part. That's why I needed to keep reading, and why I now needed to sift through every story I'd ever been told, to pour through every legend living in my mind for a hint or detail that would be Cronus's downfall.

And yet … if my mate wanted me to sit here for her, I would sit.

"You're still thinking, Kai," she chided, skimming her hands over my knees and up my thighs. "I can feel your stress, my night."

"We don't have enough time," I said, pushing through the urge to keep my fears locked up tight. She hated when I did that, and relief always bloomed through her soul whenever I confessed what was worrying me. "There's so much we need to do before we're ready to go, so many variables that could go wrong and—"

My tongue flicked out with a hiss when she leaned forward and kissed my bulge, only a few layers of fabric between us. "You're right; we're short on time. Why are we wasting it on panic?"

Anticipation tightened every nerve in my body when Haley reached for the fastening on my trousers, the zip so much faster to get undone than the knotted strings of a hundred years ago.

"You know how it goes," she said, ensnaring me in eye

contact as she reached into the gap in my pants and brushed her fingers over my shaft. I went from semi-hard to aching and desperate in a fucking second. "We plan, we examine every possible outcome and angle, we come up with an idea that can't *possibly* go wrong, we get there, and everything that can go wrong does go wrong."

A laugh puffed out of me. She had a point; I'd lost track of the amount of cock-ups we'd made over the years. Things never went according to plan. Not even according to Em's rigorous planning.

"So I'm not wasting any of the time we have tonight. I'm not taking this night of safety and calm for granted. Besides, we both know we're far better at going in guns blazing than executing a plan. Let's leave that to Em and Wane."

I smiled, and wondered how the fuck Haley was able to draw a smile from me. I'd just found out the stories I'd carried in my heart for centuries weren't stories but history, and revolved around the dictator who killed my mate—and here I was smiling.

"So what's your diabolical plan for me, then?" I asked, leaning back in the chair and trailing my stare over her bright eyes, kiss-swollen mouth, and the hardened tips of her nipples, straining like they were pleading for my touch.

"You know how you're always in charge, and I'm the submissive one?"

My cock throbbed. "Yes."

"Not today, my night," she replied, her eyes flashing with something I'd never seen before, a dark flicker of possessiveness and dominance that fit strangely with the worry in her soul. "Today, I'm going to make you forget how to think."

She pressed a kiss to the head of my cock through my underwear and I groaned. "I'm going to use my magic to slow the blood flow to your head so everything's hazy and you can't take control. Pick a safe word."

SHADOW FALL: PART ONE

My hips bucked embarrassingly off the chair. Shit. I didn't like giving up control, but I couldn't deny I was thrilled at the idea of my rose doing whatever wicked things she desired to me.

"Jynn," I said without hesitation, and devoured her answering laugh like the starved man I was.

"The name I used when I first met you," she murmured, tugging my trousers down and leaving them around my ankles. Restricting my movement, keeping me even more at her mercy. I was mortified by how turned on that made me. "Sentimental bastard."

I smiled, my lips moving slowly. Wait, all of me was moving slowly, the room growing blurry and strange. The green glow from the lamps was suddenly monstrous and threatening, and unease bled through me.

"Kai," Haley said calmly. "Look at me." I did. "I've got you. Stop stressing, just take a deep breath and relax. Let me take care of you."

It didn't come naturally, but I inhaled deeply, lifting my suddenly-heavy arm to brush the backs of my fingers over her face. It was Haley's magic making me slow. Making me easy prey for her.[2]

"Gods, look at you," she said when she tugged my underwear down, my cock jumping, aching, dripping precum all over my black shirt. I stopped caring about that when Haley wrapped her warm fingers around my shaft and squeezed. "I love this cock. You know that?"

I nodded, my head heavy and eyelids barely parted over my eyes. I forced them to stay open, desperate to see her, to watch. I sank my teeth into my bottom lip when she parted her mouth and ran her lips up and down my length, her tongue flicking out to taste the winding path of a vein. I couldn't hold back a groan when she suctioned her mouth tighter, the sensation fucking *heavenly*.

"Haley," I breathed, pleasure mixing with the floatiness in my head until I felt out of control.

"I'm right here," she promised, catching my hand and linking our fingers as her tongue swirled over my head. I grunted in surprise at the intensity of pleasure when she took me inside her mouth.

"Fuck," I breathed when she drew the divine heat of her mouth away and I realised she was only getting me slick for her hand. She gripped me firmly, making slow, loving strokes, synching each one with my hazy breaths.

Wings brushed my thighs, and I would have bucked off the damn chair if I hadn't been so drugged by her magic. Shit— holy shit, that felt insane. Goosebumps covered every place she touched, stroking me with her feathers and seeming intent on erasing all my brain function.

I understood what she meant when she gasped *too much* now. Her hand pumping me slowly, steadily, and the maddening stroke of her wings over my too-sensitive skin, mixed with the love and ownership I felt through the bond ... yeah, it was too fucking much.

"Haley," I moaned, begged, straining against the sluggish blur keeping me at her mercy.

"I can feel blood pumping faster in your cock," she told me, and my eyes slammed shut as a wave of pleasure flooded me. "Are you close?"

I nodded fast, my head spinning, all the muscles tightening in my legs, in my ass. I'd never live it down if Harvey found out I came in two fucking minutes, but with my body flush with tingling pleasure and my mate's hand pumping me, her palm squeezing whenever she slid over my tip—I couldn't hold back.

When Haley swiftly released my aching dick and sat back, stroking up and down my thighs and leaving me right on the goddamn edge, I snarled a throaty complaint. My cock jerked,

SHADOW FALL: PART ONE

desperate, pleading, but she left me there, so close but unable to come without another touch.

"Haley," I breathed, aware my tone was whining and unable to change it.

"I know, my night," she said sympathetically, and fuck if that voice didn't make even needier. My hips bucked off the chair; she pushed them back down, weakness flooding me so suddenly that I panicked—until she squeezed my hand, and I relaxed so thoroughly that I swore I floated out of my body.

"What did I say our plan for tomorrow is?" she asked, her eyes fixed on my face with burning satisfaction. *Glad you're enjoying yourself, my rose.* I wasn't sure if I said that out loud or not.

"No plan," I breathed.

She made a little displeased sound. "Clearly, I haven't done a good enough job," she murmured, and made my eyes cross when she wrapped both hands around my throbbing cock, doing this insane twisting motion that made it impossible to breathe.

"Please," I begged.

"You're so fucking hot," she groaned, leaning up to kiss me. Why was I so sensitive? Even my lips tingled when she kissed me, and my heartbeat whooshed in my ears when she sucked my bottom lip into her mouth at the same time she did that maddening double-stroke on my cock.

I tried to speak, to swear, but all that escaped was a strangled groan.

Heat poured through me like lava, scorching my balls, making my cock jolt wildly. I arched my back, desperate for her to touch me everywhere, desperate to come. When she released my mouth to cover my face in kisses, I panted, each breath laboured and gruff. My hips shot off the chair, my body arched, mouth parted as pleasure built viciously.

"What's our plan to kill Cronus?" she asked me, lips trailing down my throat.

"Who?"

Her hands moved faster on my cock, gripping so perfectly tight, and when she slid back down my body so she could wrap her lips around my tip, sucking at the same time she twisted her hands—

My whole goddamn soul ripped out of my body and I climaxed so hard I stopped breathing. Pleasure gripped my cock even tighter than Haley's hands, wringing every last drop of cum from me, demanding even more when I thought I couldn't possibly keep coming. She swallowed everything I gave her, the suction and swirling of her tongue making me cry out.

Satisfaction flowed through her soul into mine, and I resumed breathing with a hard gasp, my ass slamming back into the chair as every bit of tension tore out of my body. Limp and weak, I panted, staring at the ceiling.

It was a moment before I realised she was speaking, her voice low and soothing, her fingers stroking through my hair as I came back down to Earth. Hell. Actually, I didn't know where the fuck we were.

"Gods," I choked out.

She laughed, which seemed sadistic, but I'd probably given her the same laugh more than once. Satisfied she hadn't given me permanent brain damage, she ran her tongue over my soft cock, cleaning me up, and tucked me back into my underwear, pulling up my pants while I sat there, stunned.

When she dropped herself onto my lap and linked her arms behind my neck, I let my head fall onto her shoulder and breathed, "You are dangerous, Halwen Vakhara."

She snorted. "Don't worry, it's very mutual."

"Goddamn, Haley," I grunted, wrapping my arms around her now I could use them again.

Her laugh was entirely too smug. "Better?"

"So much better," I admitted, kissing her collarbone. "I think I need to sleep for a decade, though."

She laughed again, and the sound felt like a fucking miracle. She was here, and mine, and defiantly alive.

I'd do whatever it took to keep it that way. But first, I needed to sleep.

CHAPTER 23

HALWEN

"*M*y arm's going numb," I complained, giving Wynvail a dark look.

"You'll cope," he replied sleepily and rolled closer, his head pillowed on my forearm and his body wrapped around mine. He looked peaceful and happy, and I didn't want to move him, but *fuck* my arm was starting to hurt.

"Can you lay your head on my chest instead?" I asked, raking my fingernails through his short hair and tugging on the ends. "Please, Wyn?" I whined, appealing to his better nature. "Just for a little while?"

When he didn't even snort, I nudged his shoulder, and choked on a cry when the heat and solidity of him collapsed under my hand.

"No," I gasped, sitting up suddenly, and shaking my head over and over. Denial was a spear in my chest. I couldn't draw air.

I was covered in ashes, the grey stuff clinging to my hands, my arm, and piled on the bed in the shape of a body. *Wynvail's* body.

He—he couldn't be—he was *safe*, he was fine. Hades and Persephone saved his soul, they gave him a new body, they *saved him.*

I sobbed, covering my mouth when my bottom lip quivered, and retched when ashes brushed my lips. I could taste him, could taste the ash and death of my mate.

Shaking, I threw myself off the bed, unprepared for the sight that met me. My whole world fell apart. There wasn't one pile of ash on the bed. There were five. *Five.*

One for each of my mates.

I twisted aside and threw up, a deeper wave of nausea hitting me when the low, rumbling groan of stone on stone sounded behind me, and I realised we weren't in a bedroom. We were in the Labyrinth.

We never escaped.

I THREW MYSELF OUT OF BED, BARELY RECOGNISING THAT I WAS *in* a bed, not on the stone floor of the Labyrinth, and threw myself at the ensuite bathroom. Through a sheer miracle, I reached the toilet before I vomited, each wave of sickness clenching my stomach in painful squeezes.

Within seconds, the bathroom was full of bodies and panic, and concern flooded my soul from every bond. Tears burned their way out of my eyes and down my cheeks. I could *feel* them, all of them. Alive, not unmade.

I lifted my hand to silently ask them to back up, but I'd barely moved my fingers when a crimson pulse of magic shot from my palm and incinerated the bougie collection of shampoo bottles beside me.

Oh, gods. I didn't mean to do that.

The melted lump of plastic and shampoo smoked, destroyed. Magic rattled through me now, volatile and growing with every second. I hadn't called my power up; I didn't *want* to use it. And yet it thrummed and howled through my body, responding to the threat and terror of my nightmare.

Fucking nightmares. I hated them.

"Back up," Emlyn warned, pitching his voice low so I wouldn't hear him.[1]

"I'm not leaving," Kai hissed. "She needs me."

"She needs to release that power," Harvey disagreed, not lowering his voice. I loved him for that, my heart swelling even as I shuddered and sparked with power.

Why was there so much of it? Magic roared in my veins, thumping through my head until my mates' voices warped, and it didn't listen to any of my panicked commands to *stop*, or *calm the fuck down*.

Another pulse blasted from my hand when I tried to push to my feet, this burst of red light dissolving part of the toilet bowl. Fucker!

I'd blasted a hole through the Labyrinth with this dangerous magic, and I still didn't know *how*. But the last thing I wanted was to blow holes in our new home.

"Your magic's responding to your fear, Sugarplum," Harvey said gently, coming a single step closer. "Do you need to go outside and release it?"

Outside. Where I wouldn't hurt my mates or destroy the house.

I nodded, and before I could move towards the door, Wynvail elbowed past Wane and grabbed my waist, white light enveloping us.

No. No no no!

"Are you insane?" I screamed when the light released us in

the tall trees beside the house. I curled my hands into tight fists at my sides, shaking all over. "I could have killed you!"

Oh, gods, I could have *killed him.*

Pain and grief cut my chest, the nightmare still close enough to have its teeth in the vulnerable flesh of my heart. I could have killed him when he grabbed me; we were caught inside his power for five seconds, more than long enough for my magic to have burned a hole through his chest.

Power shattered down my arms, burning hot and endless in my gut, and I threw my hands out at the tall trees that backed onto our house. Gasps took over my breathing.

I could have lost him. Again. I came so dangerously close.

I dropped to my knees and threw up again, and it wasn't just bile that splattered the leaf-strewn ground but magic too—deep blood-red flames and power as black as the void. A chill spread through me. Was Cronus infecting me through my nightmares?

Was I ... tainted by him?

"Is that shadow moving strangely to you?" Wynvail breathed, grabbing my forearms and pulling me unceremoniously to my feet.

His body was taut, alert. I knew which shadow he meant—there was a patch of darkness slanted between the trees, interrupting the pale-dawn lilac light in a way that seemed just slightly ... off. Like it was never supposed to be here.

"He's here," Wyn gasped, a tremor moving through him and into my body.

I waited for panic to hit my system, but instead *relief* made my shoulders droop. It bled all the way through my soul, followed by a comfort I struggled to put into words. I dragged in a long breath, pretended my mouth wasn't full of the taste of bile, and smiled.

I stroked Wyn's tense arm. "It's not him. It's alright."

My jagged magic soothed as I stared at the swath of true,

sable darkness. A shadow far too dark to cut between these trees. A darkness as old as the world itself.

"Hey, Busty," I said with a casual nod of greeting. "How's it going?"

He couldn't talk to me; all he could do from wherever he existed now was watch. But apparently he still had enough power left to influence the shadows on Earth. Wait, no, in Hell. Fuck, I was losing track of where we were.

Wyn was still freaked out; he pulled me back several steps, a low sound in his throat that reminded me of Harvey. "Stay away from us. This is your only warning."

I could just picture the withering look Erebus would give my mate. I squeezed Wyn's arm and said, "This is my friend; he's cool. Not a threat."

But what was he doing here? Was he here to deliver an ominous, albeit wordless warning? That was very on brand.

Wynvail relaxed in increments. The fact he didn't slice the shadow apart with his moonlight was testament to how much he trusted me.

The back door slammed open behind us, and the rest of my mates and Verena rushed out, panicked, protective, and— in Verena's case—confused as fuck.

"I'm fine," I assured them. "I'm in control of my magic now."

Em blew out a rough breath, stalking over to me and dropping a kiss on my head before stepping back, knowing full well he'd get trampled if he didn't let the rest of my mates touch me.

"Are you okay?" Kai demanded, knocking Wynvail aside so he could drag me into a hug. "What the hell happened in there?"

"Just a nightmare," I soothed him, lifting my hand so Harvey could hold my hand. His shoulders slumped, and his eyes closed for a long moment before he held eye contact, silently asking if I was okay. Whatever he saw in my gaze calmed him enough that he didn't fight Kai for the right to hug me.

"Kai," I murmured, pulling away from my octopus-level-clingy mate with effort, searching until I found Wane's turbulent silver stare.

"I'm alright," I told him, smiling when his soul rushed against mine, seeking, checking, urgent. His gaze slid from me to the slice of darkness between the trees, acutely aware of its wrongness, but he pulled me close and laid a slow kiss on my lips despite the other presence in our back garden.

Verena was worried enough that she didn't make gagging sick noises while we kissed.

"Who is it?" Wane asked quietly, his lips brushing my ear.

"Erebus," I replied, turning my face to kiss his cheek before I stepped back, catching his hand and reaching for Harvey's, too. "Guys, that suspicious looking patch of shadows over there is my friend." I caught Kai's gaze with a smile. "Say hi to Erebus, the first shadow."

Kai's legs gave out; he sucked in a sharp breath, staring at the darkness. "How the fuck...?" he whispered, barely audible.

My mind conjured the image of a very smug looking Erebus, content with his impressive celebrity status. But he wasn't here for a social call.

"Are you here to warn us?" I asked, my nightmare rising to the surface of my brain again. A premonition? "Should we—avoid going to the prison?"

Avoid saving my friend. Fuck, it was hard to even contemplate it.

"You're talking to a shadow," Verena said under her breath, hanging close to Emlyn.

The shadow stretched further across the ground, but I didn't know what he was trying to tell me.

"Wane, can you speak to him in a secret shadow way?" I asked desperately.

My mate shook his head, his eyes wide. "Shadows don't speak, itzaia."

Alright, then. I was out of other ideas.

I squeezed their hands and let go. "Don't panic; I'll be fine."

And before they could say anything, I hot-footed it across the ground and stepped into the swath of shadow.

CHAPTER 24

$\mathcal{E}$rebus didn't speak to me, didn't offer helpful platitudes or words of wisdom. He replayed our last conversation through a crackle of static like a record player, and a deep frown cut between my brows as my ears filled with the sound of his voice.

Use your power, Halwen. All of it, every kind that lives inside you. You have more than he could ever dream to possess, even devouring most of Olympus. You have true, unbridled power, untainted by misery and pain. That's more powerful than any god he's swallowed.

That makes no sense! That was me, making a very valid point. Fuck it was weird to hear myself speak. Was that really my voice? I didn't like it. I sounded like a right twat.

Trust yourself, and don't be afraid of your power. It won't hurt you; it will only do as you bid it. You have the strength to do this, I promise you. If you need advice, I believe the most appropriate counsel is a modern term: give 'em hell, Halwen.

And that was it.

The shadow retreated without an encouraging ripple of

darkness or a foreboding looming shade. The shadow's only contribution was a very swift shove, and I stumbled back, nearly falling onto my ass when my bare foot caught on a tree root.

The warmth of pale sunlight reached my skin again and I shuddered.

My head spun. That was it? That couldn't be *it*. No fucking way. Erebus hadn't gone to all this effort just to replay a conversation that boiled down to *you got this.*

"How is that helpful?" I demanded, out of breath like I'd just finished a workout as I stared at the slant of darkness but—

Ah shit, I understood. Erebus couldn't talk to me, couldn't help me in any way except replaying what he'd told me in the past.

Trust yourself, and don't be afraid of your power.

He was here because I saw darkness in my crimson power, and it scared the shit out of me.

I expelled a sigh, and a wry smile crossed my face. "Alright, consider your message received."

I didn't know how I had a tiny tendril of darkness in me, but I had three mates descended from Erebus himself, so it wasn't hugely surprising. *Nothing to worry about. Everything's normal here, folks.*

"Thanks," I added, and hurried back to my mates before they had matching heart attacks. "I'm fine," I promised them. "I just—I saw something new in my magic when I lost control, and Erebus came to remind me not to be afraid of my power. He's like my magic tutor now. He'll probably drop by to help every now and then."

Because he was a bored busybody with nothing to do except involve himself in his family's lives. I smiled wider, at least until I turned back to the trees and found every patch of light and shadow exactly where it was meant to be.

Erebus was gone.

And since he hadn't come to warn us against saving Renna, we'd better get going. We had a prison to break into.

CHAPTER 25

HARVEY

I just met my ancestor, and I couldn't process that fact. Sure, he was a shadow between two trees, but —my whole family had come from him. I wanted nothing to do with my birth name, or any of the sick family members attached to it, but it was nice to know we had other family out there. Wane, Wynvail, and I weren't alone. There was someone out there looking out for us, someone who gave a shit.

It would have been even nicer to have backup from one of the most powerful beings to ever exist right now, because the prison where Renna was held was crawling with guards. And after hours in Hell, there was no sign of Asta anywhere, so it was just us. No deadly, volatile demon who'd kill to find her wife. No demon army. Just us.

A knot tightened in my chest.

"How do we get inside?" Kai asked, his red eyes narrowed on the wide cave mouth that led to the prison. The cave where

Emlyn told us, far too casually, Zeus had been born and hidden from Cronus. The cave where Rhea had lived, where she raised her son, where she tricked her husband. No wonder Cronus had taken control of this place and tainted it by filling it with people he planned to devour. I still wasn't sure *what* he devoured—their magic, their souls, or their meat. I didn't want to think about it.

"Distraction?" Haley suggested, pressed to my side as we laid flat on our bellies atop a rocky hill covered in annoying little stones. They'd embedded themselves in my hands, my arms, and my shoes. Between that and the fact the prison was in a deep cave whose interior was full of darkness and laden with unknowable threats ... I was a tiny bit on edge.

We could walk into anything. We might not walk out.

Wane knocked his shoulder into mine, drawing my attention. "Are you okay?" he asked quietly, while Em and Haley debated how stupid a distraction could be.

I swallowed, looking at my brother, seeing ghosts and anguish in his hard silver eyes. I didn't know how he kept going when I wanted to curl into a ball, scream into a pillow, or unleash my magic on the thirty three creepy men guarding the cave. The guards stood frozen in place, but their eyes scanned the hills, and each grasped a bronze weapon in their hand. Some were swords, others sickles, and one held a whip I didn't want Haley anywhere near. They were all eerily alike; I couldn't look at them for long before glancing away, instincts telling me something was deeply wrong with them.

And my mate was right beside me, so close to danger that my whole body thrummed with the need to grab her and run back to Hell.

"Harvey," Wane breathed.

I jerked my head in a nod, meeting my brother's eyes. "I'm fine. Just need to beat the shit out of some enemies, and I'll be good."

His gaze darkened with worry, but I glanced away, looking at the guards again. "They all have the same face," I pointed out. "Those men. They look human enough, but they have the exact same face."

Wynvail nodded, unease crossing his face. Speaking of having the same face, it was eerie how similar he looked to Wane and I. Sometimes I forgot he wasn't born at the same time as us, that he didn't grow up in the basement.

I really shouldn't have been thinking about the basement right now. Not when we had to go inside that dark, ominous cave where—

Haley laid her hand over mine on the rocky hill, and I jumped—and then settled, the frantic part of my soul quieting. Haley was here; I was safe.

I just had to keep *her* safe.

"They're creepy as fuck," Verena muttered on Wane's other side, her freckled hands clenching into fists. "Why are they just standing there? *Move,* freaks. Breathe or shift your weight or *something.*"

I agreed; their stillness was unnerving. My chest tightened.

"Cronus made Typhon create monsters for his trials," Wane murmured. "What are the chances these are something similar?"

"High," Emlyn muttered. "They're not moving. It doesn't look like they rotate; I think they stand guard twenty-four-seven."

"What are you thinking?" Haley asked, calculation in her stormy eyes. Fuck, I loved that look in her eye. I couldn't help but smile even if I felt sick with panic and dread.

She died. We didn't come close to losing her; we actually *lost* her. Was Renna worth this? I was a bastard for asking that, but I had to. If we'd only been here for her, I'd have grabbed my mate and run, but this was bigger.

This was the prophecy on her back, impossible to escape.

It was fate giving us no fucking choice. Cronus would find her no matter what we did, but we could take control here. Empty his buffet cart so he couldn't grow in power.

Deep down I knew there was no retiring from this fight, this war. That's why I was here, not running back to Hell.

Emlyn made a thoughtful sound. "There must be something in these bags to cause an explosion. What if we blow up the ground in front of them, and Haley, you slow their heartbeats while they're distracted. When they pass out, we go into the cave. And follow the plan we made last night."

Haley hiked up the strap of her satchel and smiled. My stomach both clenched with dread and fluttered with butterflies. "Wyn?"

"Harvey, do you have a jar with a purple flower in it?" Wynvail asked, glancing across Kai, Em, and Haley to meet my eyes.

I frowned and dug through the bag, blinking at the innocent looking plant. Wynvail's grin was mildly alarming when I drew it out.

"Everyone, shield your eyes. Harvey, fill the jar with sun magic and throw it at the guards."

"What is it?" Verena asked, eyeing the jar covetously.

"Some mad scientist's experiment," Wynvail replied quietly, his eyes on the cave. There was no sign of movement inside, but he watched it like he was as suspicious as I was. There was a prison inside, and Cronus's most high profile prisoners were locked up here. It might have looked like an abandoned cave[1] but it was anything but abandoned inside. A tremor went through me, but I locked my body to control it.

Locke isn't inside, I snarled at myself. *He's dead. Wynvail killed him.*

Yet, my stomach twisted, and I could feel the heat of his breath on the back of my neck, could smell his wine and cigarette smoke scent.

Haley tightened her hand around mine, and I sucked down a breath of fresh air. I tasted dirt, minerals, and rainclouds—no smoke and wine. He was dead.

"Blowing shit up can be cathartic," Wane whispered, startling a quiet laugh out of me.

So I pulled my hand out from under Haley's and sank into the boiling pool of my magic. It had been warm and comforting once, the soft brush of sunlight, but now it was a light that scalded, that took no prisoners.

I screwed the lid off the jar and pressed my palm over it, my magic rising effortlessly. Emotions were the key to controlling power—and losing control of it. There was never a moment when I wasn't full of rage and grief and fear, never a moment when my magic wasn't ready.

I filled the jar until it glowed as bright as a sunbeam. It was easy, effortless.

"Shield your eyes," I reminded everyone, and waited until all their heads ducked—watching Verena the longest, expecting her to rebel and surprised when she didn't.

Wane was right. Rearing my arm back and hurling the jar full of magic at the cave was cathartic. I threw my rage along with it, and when the glass shattered upon impact with the ground, it took some of my fear with it, too. The purple flower was visible for a split second as a luminous violet glow before sunlight erupted like the heart of an explosion.

Holy shit. A laugh bubbled up my throat, satisfaction and viciousness driving out my fear for a moment. A plume of light erupted so far and high that guards were thrown in a dozen different directions. Damn. I understood why Wynvail collected all this shit now.

I shielded my eyes to track where they were thrown, and the second the light faded to a safe level, I pointed them out to my mate. The grin she wore brought my butterflies back.

But within a minute the guards were unconscious, and it

was time to move. My heart picked up again, blood roaring in my ears.

"I'm right beside you," Wane reminded me, earning an exasperated glance. "What?"

"How are you not affected?" I demanded, pushing to my feet and skidding down the hill with my mate and brother. Kai raced ahead, the air quivering with power and scattering tiny stones around him.

Wane laughed, low and rolling—a laugh of warning. "Not affected? I'd rather open a hundred wounds on my body than go inside that cave." His gaze drifted to Haley, and mine followed. "But I'd follow her anywhere."

I sighed, my shoulders slumping. "So would I."

"You guys are sickly sweet," Verena remarked, her nose wrinkled as she eavesdropped. "I need to blow shit up."

"Time check," Emlyn called in the deep, serious voice that sent me back to a hundred different memories. A hundred different jobs. Locke had been hunting us then, but now he was dead. They were *both* dead.

"Nine, exactly," I answered, glancing at my watch, my stomach flopping. Oh gods, we were really doing this.

"We've got two minutes," Kai pointed out, and picked up his pace, racing full-pelt down the hill.

I had a really, really bad feeling about this. I was going to throw up.

Sunlight pouring through my veins, I twisted towards my mate, my mouth open to beg her to run away with me forever.

But she kicked off the ground and a sharp air whipped me from a powerful wingbeat, blowing my hair off my shoulders and into my face. Fuck. She stirred balmy air into sharp wind as she flew, and I had no chance of catching up to her as she flew ahead.

Emlyn leapt into the air too, but I remained on the ground, my entire soul screaming at me to follow them. I wasn't leaving Wane. I wouldn't be another reminder that his wings had been severed from him.

Shit, the cave was *huge* from up close, the opening three times my height and as wide as one of Wynvail's fancy houses. It was entirely black inside. My stomach cramped tighter, nausea flowing through me.

Haley paused in the air, glancing back, but I threw my arm up and gestured for her to fly, to race towards the cave. We needed to get inside at 09:02, and we were running out of time. It was 09:01 already.

"One minute," I yelled, my chest tightening until I could barely breathe. I swivelled my head, counting—Wane, Verena, Kai, Wynvail, Emlyn, Haley. All here. All safe.

But for how long?

I'd voted to come here, to get Renna to safety, but right here, in this moment, I wished I'd voted against it. We were racing right back into danger, and even though our safety had been tentative and breakable at best, we *had* been safe.

What were we doing?

I caught my breath when Emlyn and Haley plunged into the true black of the cave.

My heart stopped beating for a second of pure, undiluted panic. There was no turning back now.

I HOPE YOU LOVED THE FIRST PART OF SHADOW FALL. THE BOOK was just too humongous to contain to a single volume, and I didn't want you to wait six months between installments of Haley's series.

The second part of Shadow Fall and the final book in the *Kissed by Brimstone* series is available to preorder now and will be with you very soon! Fair warning, this book was the calm before the storm. I hope you're ready for an epic showdown.

Thank you so much for sticking with this series. I love these characters so, so much and it makes me happy to know you do, too.

See you in the next book!

Leigh x

FREE VAMPIRE ROMANCE STORY!

Hybrid's Curse is a stand-alone paranormal romance.

As a vampire-witch hybrid who can never be killed, Emilio is used to pain and suffering. But when Aislin, an innocent faerie healer, is kidnapped because of him, Emilio will do anything to stop her suffering too. Especially because she's been dreaming of him for seven years, and claims to be his mate.

If you love romantic stories with a healthy dose of suspense, and pairings of dark, gloomy men and sunny, optimistic women, you'll enjoy this happily-ever-after story.

JOIN MY MAILING LIST FOR YOUR FREE STORY

SIGNED LEIGH KELSEY BOOKS!

You can find all my available print copies in my online book store, plus books from my cowrites and pen-names, **and all orders come with swag and a dedication from yours truly.**

VISIT THE STORE: https://payhip.com/snarkystabbybooks

FIND THESE OTHER PSYCHOS BY LEIGH KELSEY!

Feared by Monsters: A stand-alone twisted paranormal romance

Killers and Kings series
(Complete Twisted Paranormal Demon RH)
Crazed Candy
Sweet Violence
Sugar Rush

Kissed By Brimstone series
(Twisted Paranormal Demon RH)
Hellborn Angel
Midnight Descent
Eternal Night
Cursed Dawn
Shadow Fall: Part 1
Shadow Fall: Part 2

Rebels and Psychos Duet
(Complete Twisted Paranormal RH)
Complete Series Box Set
Killer Crescent
Blood Wolf

Sick and Twisted series
(Twisted Death Gods RH)
All Hallows Night

JOIN MY READER GROUP!

To get news about upcoming releases before anywhere else, and early access to my books, come join my Leigh Kelsey's Paranormal Den group over on Facebook!

ABOUT LEIGH KELSEY

Leigh Kelsey writes about psychos with questionable morals and addictions to shiny, stabby objects, but she's perfectly harmless, she swears. She can be found in Yorkshire, England listening to K-Pop, watching serial killer documentaries, and writing as much spicy paranormal romance as she possibly can in a day.

LEIGH KELSEY

WHERE THE MEN ARE *PSYCHO* BUT THE WOMEN ARE *WICKED*

f

COMPLETE TWISTED PARANORMAL RH SERIES

If a secret wolf society thinks they can take me down, they've got another thing coming. There's a reason they call me Graves.

It's not my fault I'm a psychopath. What else would happen to someone who witnessed her sister's murder? Without magic in my arsenal like the rest of my family, I have to rely on other methods: sharp knives, stealth, and killer instincts. And hey, killing pays the bills.

NOTES

CHAPTER 1

1. Not Wane, obviously. As far as I could tell, the man was a saint and had never done anything wrong to anyone.
2. Very picturesque, I'd be sure to pick up a postcard.
3. Wasn't it a tad fucking cliché that death was black and empty? Let me guess, if I wanted to move on, I had to follow a white light?
4. Probably because I died. Give me a break.

CHAPTER 3

1. Also dark grey, but definitely, undeniably pink.
2. He tried. He failed.
3. Which actually happened. Later, I found out he'd kissed his new girl while we were still courting, and I'd kneed him in the balls. My dad gave me a very stern look for being so violent in public, and in private gave me a big grin and told me I should have pushed him into a puddle too, so everyone knew he was filth.

CHAPTER 7

1. He couldn't. He only got up to six.
2. I was hungry.
3. Let's be real, was there any part of me that *didn't* have a praise kink?
4. Although, relatable, right...?

CHAPTER 8

1. No hero swept in to help *me* out, I noticed. That was fine. I was a self-sufficient demon who definitely didn't throw Haley a petulant look.

CHAPTER 9

1. It was everything I wanted to give my rose, and I hated Wynvail for it.

CHAPTER 10

1. Okay, one I stole in Iarlon.
2. Fuck dying. Dying sucked.

CHAPTER 11

1. No seriously. *Virgin.* Don't tell her.

CHAPTER 12

1. I was very proud of that disarray. It was some of my best work.
2. My boobs were cold now. Bastard.
3. He was literally gods' gift to demonkind, but if I pointed that out, it would go straight to his head.
4. I liked seeing that smugness on him, but don't you dare repeat that.
5. That was uncalled for! Totally off the mark. Not even remotely true... How *dare* he?

CHAPTER 13

1. Aspirational.
2. I was legitimately considering entering them into eating competitions now we were going crime-free. We'd make a killing.
3. If you're thinking I stole them from Wynvail, you'd be correct.
4. You're welcome, Wane, glad to be of service.

CHAPTER 14

1. Unless it was Haley. Then I'd just withhold orgasms; I wasn't about to punch the light of my life.

CHAPTER 15

1. Not a euphemism.
2. I appreciated the sentiment, but I could have done without the saliva gleaming on my flagstones. Wynvail's low mutter behind me said he was fuming.

CHAPTER 17

1. Hopefully the grey ones. A little silver was distinguishing and rakish, but I'd started noticing more and more lately. Another year of this stress and I could get a perm and a blue rinse.

CHAPTER 18

1. For future reference, when someone tells you to *look* at something, don't *touch* it like some idiot did.

CHAPTER 19

1. When should I tell him this was *our* path, and our new home?

CHAPTER 21

1. And yes, I was still using inverted commas when it came to that word.
2. Mostly because I recognised it as my own.
3. Trauma? I hardly know her.

CHAPTER 22

1. In theory, if any of us dumbasses were smart enough. Maybe Em. Probably Em.
2. That should not have been as thrilling as it was.

CHAPTER 23

1. Spoiler: I still heard him.

CHAPTER 25

1. If you ignored the thirty-three robotic guards

www.ingramcontent.com/pod-product-compliance
Lightning Source LLC
Chambersburg PA
CBHW030255200626
46816CB00002BA/655